CONTENTS

THE THURSDAY WRITERS CLUB ANTHOLOGY

by

Phil Appleby

Julian Cadman

Peter Lucas

Julia Peers

Kate Sharp

and

Ester Spiller

Book Cover by Kindle Cover Creator

1st edition 2024

PROLOGUE

Writing fiction is a very strange thing to do, it's one of those professions, like acting and politics, where you lie to people, and get praised for it.

Don't act surprised, you know we're lying, and you're very happy about it. In fact that's why you're reading this. Nobody wants unspeakable monsters from the dungeon dimensions to pierce our thin veil of reality. But give us a hot cuppa, a comfy chair and a purring cat and we'll read about it for hours.

I'm so thankful that this group of thoughtful, intelligent people keep coming back, for me to keep cajoling them further into this life of lies.

Since we're on the subject of sin, I should probably also admit to pride. This I must humbly confess, dear reader, is a sin that I have fallen victim to. I am proud. So very, very proud to be associated with this work, with these classes I tutor, with this amazing group of writers that I get to hang out with, and laugh with, and share with every week. I am so incredibly proud to be part of this journey of discovery. I have learned more than I've taught.

Luckily, I can pin killing their darlings on someone else...

PHIL APPLEBY

Phil worked for 29 years as a technical writer and editor for IBM, taking early retirement in 2015.

Phil has always enjoyed writing and worked as a theatre reviewer on The Leamington Spa Courier for two years. More recently, he co-authored a military history book, *The RAF Armourers: Safely Making Aircraft Dangerous Since the First World War*, which was published in September 2023.

Phil was born and brought up in Northumberland, and now lives on the south coast in Lymington with his Japanese wife and their daughter. Away from work he enjoys playing golf and walking in the New Forest. He is also a renowned Scrabble player, winning the UK National Championship in 1991 and representing England in the World Scrabble Championship on seven occasions.

His contributions to this anthology are based on class homework assignments. He continues to work on several more substantial pieces of work that he hopes will one day become international best-sellers.

DRABBLES

Theme: This piece of homework involved writing one or more drabbles. A drabble is a piece of fiction that is exactly 100 words in length, and often ends with a little twist.

Revenge

I like to dismember corpses in the kitchen. The blood stains can easily be cleared up afterwards by wiping the floor tiles. Once I used the living room instead, which was very messy. Carpets and blood-stained corpses are not a good combination. I'll stick to the kitchen from now on. Today's corpse was fun. I managed to detach the head from the body, which is always particularly satisfying.

Of course I know that Jon won't be happy, but this is entirely his fault. What does he expect if he forgets to fill my bowl with Felix before going to bed?

Avoiding Detection

I'm sure there is no-one following me, but better just check... Yep, all clear. I reach up and carefully extract the metal container. I open it. Inside is a yellowing piece of paper, and several small items. Nothing valuable. I look for money, but there isn't any. There is a pen, but it doesn't work. They never do. Fortunately, I brought my own. I write on the paper and return it to the box. Another quick look around, then I place the container back where I found it. I do love geocaching, but you must make sure no-one sees you.

Taking Orders

I've never liked being told what to do. There's a part of me that wants to rebel, to do exactly the opposite. I know it doesn't make sense, but that's how it is. Also, and I know this is going to sound sexist, I'm really not happy about taking orders from a woman. Particularly a woman who sounds like such a know-it-all.

I can sense she's about to give me another instruction. But I just need to swallow my male pride and do what I'm told. Here we go… "In 500 feet, turn right at the roundabout onto Hill Lane."

Never-Ending Nightmare

I feel as though I'm going mad. I'm trapped, strapped in, unable to escape. Most of what I'm seeing makes little sense, and the unremitting, repetitive, haunting sound is a nightmare. I feel that it will remain in my head forever, taunting me, forcing me to relive this terrible experience. And there are so many other, more enjoyable things I could be doing instead. But finally, thankfully, it's over. At last, I can start to relax.

Then I hear a small voice next to me, that of my five-year-old daughter: "Dad, can we go on 'It's a Small World' again?"

Moment of Truth

Millie is frightened. This man sitting next to her is extremely intimidating. He's tall and broad, with a strong aura of authority. Perhaps an ex-serviceman? But it's the silence that really bothers Millie. He's barely spoken to her, and the few words he's uttered have been terse and unfriendly. And now he's saying nothing. Just looking down – but at what? She yearns to run away, but what good would that do?

Finally, the man looks up at Millie, and smiles. She smiles back, nervously. Then he speaks. "Miss Richards, I'm pleased to say that you've passed your driving test. Congratulations."

Sense of Loss

Paul opens the bedroom door. Looks at the bare mattress–no sheets or duvet. No-one will be sleeping there tonight. The room feels cold and empty.

He closes the door and walks downstairs. The house seems so quiet. He can feel tears welling up. Life will never be the same again. He knows that he has to eat some food, but he has no appetite. Just a deep sense of loss.

She's gone. His precious daughter. Gone. To university. It's just Paul and Marie now. Right on cue, Marie calls him. "Dinner's ready, Paul. Can you bring in the wine?"

The Joy of Fugu

Theme: A piece influenced by food. My story was based, very loosely, on a trip to Japan with my wife.

Robert was scared. He knew that his Japanese fiancée's father wasn't overly pleased about his daughter marrying an Englishman, but surely he wouldn't go this far? That said, Haruko's father was a formidable character – small in stature, but a man of considerable authority, reflecting his role as a senior manager in a large construction company. What lengths might he go to in order to prevent the marriage?

This was Robert's first trip to Japan, and despite his misgivings he had to admit that up to now he'd been looked after extremely well by Haruko's parents. They had taken him to see Mount Fuji, and several famous temples. And they had made sure that he got to sample some of Japan's famous cuisine. Prior to this trip his experience of Japanese food had been confined to Wagamama, but during the past week his eyes, and his stomach, had witnessed all kinds of culinary delights.

The most memorable meal had been at one of Tokyo's top teppanyaki restaurants. Haruko's father had booked a private dining room, and their chef had cooked each course on the teppanyaki grill in front of the family. One of the courses was tiger prawns. Robert realised that they would be exceptionally fresh when he saw them being brought in, still wriggling after being removed from their tank. The chef held them down on the grill with a large knife, while they writhed in their death throes. A couple of minutes later they were on his plate, ready to eat – and he had never eaten anything tastier.

But today was a very different prospect. Today they were about to eat lunch in an authentic fugu restaurant. Robert had done a bit of Googling about fugu, and he rather wished he hadn't. He now knew that fugu, also known as puffer fish, was lethally poisonous if it was cooked incorrectly. What he also discovered was that if you are unlucky enough to suffer from fugu poisoning, you don't lose consciousness, but you slowly die from asphyxiation – so you sit there knowing you're dying and can do nothing about it. And there is no known antidote. In its wisdom, the UK, and the rest of Europe, had banned the consumption of fugu because it was so dangerous. You will never find puffer fish on a Wagamama menu.

It got worse. His searches revealed that there had been a recent death in Tokyo where a client had been poisoned at a fugu restaurant. No doubt this tragedy had been the consequence of an unfortunate accident, but what if Haruko's father had paid the chef to "inadvertently" fail to remove some of the poison from Robert's portion of fugu?

The first course arrived. Sashimi, with translucent slices of fugu on top of rice. Robert waited until everyone else had eaten some before tentatively picking up a piece with his chopsticks. He was pleasantly surprised. Not bad at all. Then there was a starter – smoked fugu with a side salad. Delicious! And finally, the main course, a fugu stew with stir-fried vegetables. Weirdly, it tasted rather like a chicken casserole. Almost the same as one of his mother's...

And suddenly Robert knew that he wasn't going to die. Everything was going to be fine. In fact, it was going to be better than fine. It was going to be perfect. Just like his fugu lunch.

My Scrabble Bag

Theme: Memories triggered by an everyday object.

I was in the attic last week, searching for a long-lost card table. I moved some Christmas decorations, and there it was – not the card table, but a large, blue bag, with the letters "PJA" sewn onto the front. It had two fabric handles, also sewn on. One of the handles was slightly frayed. It was a large bag, large enough to hold a personalised Scrabble board with racks and tiles, a chess clock, and lots of customised score sheets. There was even a neat little pocket for pens. I picked it up, put my hand inside, as I'd done so many times before, and felt the emptiness.

My wife had made the bag for me, shortly after we got married. She knew that I was a serious Scrabble player, and clearly found it painful watching me pack my assorted accessories into a couple of Waitrose carrier bags as I headed off to a tournament. The Scrabble bag was a wonderful gift, one that made me feel special. It was something I truly treasured.

Over the years the bag, together with its contents, was very well travelled. There were the local events, on the Isle of Wight, and in Bournemouth and Southampton. The Isle of Wight was a favourite; there was just enough time to squeeze in a quick practice game on the ferry to Cowes. Then there were the major competitions, the National Scrabble Championship in central London, and the Masters tournament, attended by only the very best – the top 16 players in the UK. And of course there were the World Championships...

* * *

Suddenly I'm back in Kuala Lumpur, Malaysia. It's 2003, and I've won my last seven games. With just three games to play I'm in third place. Three more wins and I'm in the Final, with the chance to carve my name into Scrabble history. I'm playing Andrew Perry, a fellow Brit. Very young, just out of his teens, and very tall. A top player, cool and confident. But I know I can beat him.

It's a tight game. Lots of pressure. Nerves tingling. Few openings. But I start to pull ahead. VIXEN for 48 gives me a 92-point lead, with tiles running out. I can feel the tension–I'm so close to the crucial win. Then Andrew plays FOEDARIE for 71, and on the next move he puts down CONTUSED for 81. Suddenly I'm 40 points behind. Too late for a comeback. I lose the game by 16 points. I feel crushed. I lose my final two games too, and finish in 14th place. One of the many also-rans.

* * *

I put the Scrabble bag down. It's no longer a part of my life. I dropped out of tournament Scrabble in 2009 and will never go back. I had come to realise that my standards were slipping, and I hated not being able to compete at the highest level. And I missed my young daughter every time I headed off for a tournament. The bag is my past. The attic is where it belongs.

I climb down the stepladder, back into the present.

Homeless

Theme: A first-person character vignette.

I never imagined I'd be homeless. Homeless was something that happened to other people. Not people like me. For Christ's sake, I've got a university degree. How on earth did I end up like this?

I'm William, by the way. Although most people knew me as Will. Now people only know me as that sad bloke who sits in the street under the archway, trying to keep warm with the help of a woolly hat and a threadbare rug. I wonder what they think of me? Do they question how I ended up here? Do they think of what I might have been, before I joined the ranks of the homeless? I very much doubt it. Most of them turn away. No-one wants to look me in the eye. They don't want to be faced with the thought: "In another life, that could have been me." The same thought that regularly haunts me.

There are other homeless people around here who shout out to passers-by: "Hey! You! Can you spare me a pound?" I never do that. I remember in the past, when I was one of those passers-by, the beggars disgusted me. I thought they were dirty, lazy good-for-nothings. And I always thought that if I did give them a quid, they'd just spend it on cigarettes or booze. I may be homeless, but I'm not a beggar. I'd rather die than beg.

In case you're wondering, the place where I live now isn't my hometown. I'd hate to see anyone I know. Anyone from my past. I left my hometown when I deserted my squalid little flat. I owed rent money, lots of money. Then I lost my job. I had to get away, to somewhere where no-one knew me. Where no-one would find me.

Like I said earlier, I'm not going to beg for food, but I still need to eat. Luckily there's a church in the town where I can get lunch. Every day they provide some cooked food. Nothing fancy, but enough to get me through the rest of the day. The people who run the food stall, John and Kathy, are nice, and they're happy to talk to me. The things we talk about aren't the kinds of things that most people would expect homeless people like me to be interested in. Things like the environment, and what's going on in the world. My degree was in Geography, so I know what I'm talking about. And there are always old newspapers lying round so I can keep up with the latest news. It's strange really. In the church I feel welcome, and I think John and Kathy genuinely like me.

Unlike my parents. They disowned me a long time ago. I've let them down. I've failed. We haven't spoken to each other in years. And yet... They're regular churchgoers. Who knows – maybe they're running a lunch club at their church, supporting their local down-and-outs? Talking to people just like me, people whose luck has run out.

The Bird Table

Theme: A first-person piece based on an inanimate object.

I guess we all end up here eventually. At the local waste recycling centre. I wonder what I'll be recycled as. A chest of drawers? A gate? Whatever it is, I don't think I'll enjoy it as much as my last life. There's something magical about being a bird table.

I lived in the middle of the lawn at a country cottage. My human family included two large people, and two small ones. I used to see my human family mainly when they left the cottage and walked up the path to the car. I didn't like it when they came out of the cottage, because my main family, my more important family, my birds, would fly away.

I really loved my birds. So many different types used to come and eat. I particularly liked the finches – I had chaffinches, greenfinches, gold finches, bullfinches... And of course I loved the robins. They had a self-confidence and cheekiness that made them extra special. One of them – I called him Jack – used to come almost every day. I always recognised him because there was a feather on his head that stuck out at a funny angle.

I think my most regular visitors were the blue tits, although the tit that I best remember was very different. He turned up one day and started nibbling away at some fresh bird seed. He was quite small and stocky, with a black head and a white neck. Not the prettiest bird who'd come to visit me.

I looked over to the cottage and could see one of the large people – the one with no hair – looking out through the window. I noticed he was getting very excited. He was taking photographs too. It turned out that this new bird was a willow tit, which is apparently very rare, particularly where we lived. For a few days lots of visitors came to the cottage, many of them with large cameras. But then the willow tit disappeared, and so did all the visitors.

Things didn't always go perfectly. Sometimes the large people forgot to give me any fresh seeds, so most of the birds would stop coming. Or the whole family would go away, so that there was no fresh seed for two or three weeks. That seemed to happen a lot in the summer. Happily, it was at a time when there were lots of other things for the birds to eat, so it didn't matter too much. And several of my favourite birds, including Jack, would still drop by to say hello.

There was also a nasty incident with a cat. I'd seen it watching me and my bird visitors. Then suddenly it leapt up onto me, and somehow managed to catch one of the blue tits. All that was left were a few feathers, trembling in the breeze. It was horrible!

I thought that this life would last forever but eventually I got old, and a bit weather-beaten, and rather mouldy. So now I'm in bin number 6, along with lots of other old bits of wood, feeling slightly sorry for myself.

And then I see a robin, sitting on the corner of the bin, looking over at me – and I spot that wonky feather on his head. It's Jack! He hops onto me, tilts his head, and sings a little song. He's come to say goodbye.

Be Careful What You Wish For

Theme: Two diary entries, separated over time.

Friday 19th October, 2012

I feel really bad for Jake. When he came home from school, he asked about the sixth form Geography field trip to Dartmoor. All of his friends are going, so he's desperate to go too. But right now we can't afford it. I hate the fact that I lost my job. I hate the fact that we've had to beg with the mortgage company to delay our latest payment. I hate the fact that instead of our usual steak and chips on a Friday evening, tonight we're eating cheesy pasta.

Things aren't going great with Jenny either. She's trying to be patient and sympathetic, but I can tell that she's finding me tough to cope with. And I can understand why. I can't help feeling angry and bitter, and I probably take it out on her. Well, I can hardly go out and discuss it over a beer with my mates, when we can't afford to buy a decent meal. Life is pretty shit at the moment.

I know it's stupid, but I bought four EuroMillions tickets for tonight's draw. It's one of those huge rollover jackpots – well over £100 million. Of course I won't tell Jenny about the tickets. Well, unless I get lucky.

Friday 21st October, 2022

Jake phoned earlier this evening. He seemed unhappy about the estate I bought him in Tanzania. I thought it was just what he wanted, but it seems that it's a bit too remote. What do you expect in Tanzania? And he has lots of lions, ostriches and giraffes to keep him company. You can never please some people.

In fact it was a bad day all round. I had to sack one of

the gardeners, because he made some lewd comments about Natasha. He even implied that he's been sleeping with her. OK, she's twenty-five years younger than me, but she wouldn't do that – would she?

Then there are the problems with the house. In retrospect I wish I'd bought a more modern place, but I couldn't resist the prospect of living in a Grade 2 listed mansion. And it seemed a snip at £10 million. The heating system is particularly flaky, and with winter looming I'm going to have to get a team of people in to get it sorted. More work. More disruption.

But the thing that bothers me most is the dodgy characters I keep seeing – usually young guys in hoodies, who seem to be checking the place out. Obviously I've got CCTV cameras all over the place, but if anything, that makes it worse. If you don't know there are dodgy characters around, you don't think of them. Whereas I end up lying awake at night, listening out for suspicious noises downstairs.

It's at times like this I really miss Jenny. She could be difficult, but she was very organised and rational. Not like Natasha.

To tell you the truth, I often find myself wishing I'd never won the lottery. I'm sure I could have got a new job, enjoyed the odd night out with my mates, watched *Doc Martin* with Jenny or *Match of the Day* with Jake… Life used to be simple. And a simple life can be very special.

Ludmila's Café

Theme: Same place, different times

Bakhmut, Ukraine: May 2019

Ludmila stands outside her eponymous café, looking out across the nearby park. You would never guess she was a grandmother; her hair is light brown, with a reddish tinge, and she is still fit and healthy.

She opened the café ten years ago, after her husband died. Her son Mykyta and his wife Elena now do the bulk of the work, preparing the food and serving the customers. Most of them are regulars, and many have known Ludmila and her family for many years. The café decor is simple, but very welcoming. Inside, the wooden tables and chairs are painted white, and local artworks adorn the pale-pink walls. There are more tables on the pavement outside, and all are occupied. It's a lovely, late-Spring day, and the locals are relishing the sunshine and warmth after the long winter months.

The trees in the park look fresh and hopeful, their new leaves a vibrant green. In the distance, at the other side of the park, Ludmila can just about see the school which her grandchildren, twin girls, attend. Possibly they're improving their reading and writing skills; more likely they're teasing each other and getting into trouble with their teacher. Ludmila smiles. There is so much to look forward to.

Bakhmut, Ukraine: May 2023

An elderly lady walks slowly up the street. She is very thin, with wispy grey hair. It's the first time she's been outside for several days. In the distance she can hear gunfire. The invading Russian forces claim to have control of the city, although the Ukrainian army is continuing to fight. Nowhere is safe, but the area next the park feels safer than most.

She stops outside a boarded-up building. The sign on the wall is still there: 'Ludmila's Café'. Her café. She's glad that it's boarded up. The Russians smashed all the furniture, and painted graffiti on the walls. Better to remember it as it was, rather than seeing it as it is now.

Almost everyone she used to know has left Bakhmut. All her customers have gone. Elena and the children are now in the UK, but she knows nothing of what they're doing. There are no means of communication. No ways to talk to the outside world. Sometimes she thinks that she should have left too, but this is her home. This is where she has always lived.

She moves on. The reason she left the relative safety of her basement apartment wasn't to visit her café. Further up the street, she opens a small gate leading into a cemetery. She walks past the old gravestones, to an area full of new, smaller stones, placed for Ukrainian soldiers who have died trying to defend their city. She finds the one marked: 'Mykyta Bilenko', cries silent tears, and prays. For a short while, she is not alone.

Millennium Vows

Theme: Same time, different places

Prologue: 31st December 1975 – 23:59

Woolington's favourite pub, the Amber Inn, is packed as the countdown begins to another year of hope and opportunity. Five young men from the village sit around a table, waiting to raise their pints of beer to see in the New Year. Most are 18. There's just young Billy who hasn't yet celebrated his coming of age. He's a shy lad who feels slightly out of place and hasn't contributed much to the conversation, most of which has revolved around football and a group of noisy girls in the corner of the pub who are surprisingly scantily dressed given the time of year. But he's thrilled to be there, to have been invited along.

The other young men are Matt, bright and self-confident, a first-year student at Manchester University; Pete, who left school at 16 and works on a local building site; Roger, who did unexpectedly badly in his A levels and doesn't quite know what to do next; and Darren, who has lots of imaginative ideas for becoming rich.

It's Matt who raises his voice above the hubbub: "Okay guys, I know we probably won't keep in touch over the years, but let's make a vow. In twenty-five years' time, we'll see in the Millennium together in the last pub in England, at Land's End. Everyone up for it?" Five glasses are raised in agreement, as the midnight chimes ring out in the nearby village church.

31st December 1999 – 23:59: Woolington church yard

Close to the church, and illuminated by the lights of the Amber Inn opposite, a simple tombstone tells its short, sad story: "Peter

Westwood. Born: January 15th, 1957. Died: November 20th, 1983. Very much missed by his family and friends." Nearby graves are adorned with flowers, accompanied by hand-written messages. Pete's grave has none, and has remained untouched since his mother died four years ago. He's gone, and largely forgotten.

31st December 1999 – 23:59: Durham Prison

Darren looks at his watch. Less than a minute to go. He knows that, come midnight and the chimes of Big Ben, most of the inmates will bang the inside of their cell doors for several minutes. Is it a celebration? Or is it a desperate plea for release from the monotony of prison life? Whatever the reason, he won't join in. He's not like them. He's different. He was just unlucky. OK, so maybe he did break the law, but who has he ever harmed? Well, apart from the pensioners he conned out of their life savings.

31st December 1999 – 23:59: Newcastle City Centre

Shivering uncontrollably, Roger pulls his shabby blanket around him. He hates this time of year. It's never fun being homeless, but the middle of winter is the worst.

What on earth went wrong? He's not stupid, and he's not lazy. He could have had a nice, stable, fulfilling life. Like everyone else. But maybe not. Perhaps he was always destined to fail–from the moment he screwed up his A levels.

Still, at least he has a can of Newcastle Brown Ale, donated by a kind passer-by who cheerfully wished him a Happy New Year. He takes a sip, remembering that vow from 25 years ago. He shouldn't be here; he should be at Land's End with his old friends.

31st December 1999 – 23:59: Heston House, near York

The large drawing room at Heston House is packed with people, mainly friends from work and their families. Everyone has a champagne glass in their hands, although for Matt's children, Evie and William, the drink of choice is apple juice rather than finest Dom Perignon.

The Millennium is a time for reflection and, at 43, Matt is more than happy with how life has turned out. After graduating with First Class Honours in the very new discipline of Computer Science, he accepted a job with IBM before starting his own software company. He now employs forty people, has a beautiful wife and two lovely children, and lives in a magnificent mansion. What more could he want? His modest upbringing in a small Northumberland village is now a distant memory; he's moved on to bigger and better things.

31st December 1999 – 23:59: The First & Last Inn, Land's End

Billy sits on his own at the bar, with an almost-empty pint glass in front of him. He feels sad, angry, confused. What happened to them?

He'd arrived in Land's End six hours ago, excited and full of anticipation. After checking into his B&B, he'd wandered over to the pub around 8 o'clock, expecting to see at least one of them already at the bar. He wasn't certain that he'd recognise his old friends, not having not seen any of them for over twenty years, but he knew they would somehow find each other. But no-one was there. And in the four hours since, no-one had come. He'd even bagged a table for them, and told several people who'd asked, "Is anyone sitting here?" that his mates were on their way.

But eventually he'd given up and retreated to a stool at the end of the bar. Maybe they were never intending to come? Or perhaps they were sitting in a pub at the other end of the country, laughing about the trick they'd played on "little Billy"?

Everyone else in the pub is having a good time as they wait to see in the Millennium, and Billy can sense their glances towards him – pity mainly, but with a bit of contempt mixed in. What kind of sad little jerk sits on his own in a pub on such a special night? He's asking himself the same question. Why on earth has he come all the way to Land's End? He'd been invited to several parties, but instead he'd driven for seven hours to be here. And for what?

He empties his glass and walks out of the door, as the midnight chimes ring out at the village church.

JULIAN CADMAN

Why Julian was born remains a mystery; but we do know he was raised just outside Reading.

Following a career in the City, rising to assistant Hole Punch Emptier, he took early retirement when pre-punched paper was introduced. The love of paper still in his heart, he sought something new to channel his innate incompetency into.

When the origami class folded, and his paper aeroplane display team failed to get off the ground, he turned a new page and took up creative writing.

Having written several award-winning deserving shopping lists, he's currently working on an author bio for an anthology...

Room with a View

Just in time! What did the receptionist say... room six? Yep – here we are.

"Barry? Ummm... you're not on my register. Never mind. You've two minutes behind the screens to arrange and then reveal your display, and we'll get to work."

Two minutes! Display? I'm a human being too lady! Try pruning this scenery and giving an artiste room to work, eh? Oh well... here goes!

"WHAT THE DICKENS ARE YOU DOING MAN?!"

"Er... I'm Barry, the Life Drawing model."

"This is blind judging for our speed Flower Arranging class. Life Drawing's room nine. Someone fetch Gladys some water..."

The Day (Or Should That Be Night..?) Halloween Died

The door creaked open, as Wanda entered a place she'd never expected to visit. A place promising opportunity, yet capable of crushing dreams. A place slowly succumbing to the darkness of the late autumnal afternoon.

A bead of sweat dripped onto the cold hard floor.

She watched it vanish.

"Good afternoon, you must be Mrs Witch. Please, take a seat. I'm Liz," said the job centre supervisor. "Now, having studied your C.V. it's not going to be easy finding what you're looking for in today's market. Breaking into T.V. is never easy..."

"...because of my age? And I'm a woman?"

"That's not what I'm saying, Mrs Witch. But it's important to manage one's expectations and, whilst I can't promise anything, I'll make some enquiries. Please — go and sit over there," said Liz, pointing back towards the entrance. "And please don't leave your broomstick in front of the fire exit. There's an umbrella stand behind you."

"Hi Wanda!" said Sienna, as Wanda settled into the seat next to her.

"Oh! Hello, Sienna," replied Wanda, "I didn't expect to see you."

"No choice, Wanda, my career's vanishing away before me. As ghosts can't press keypads, we have to buy white bedsheets from actual department stores. But you can hardly find one nowadays — honestly, the high street's becoming like a... oh, you get the picture. Anyhow, Liz over there is..."

"...managing your expectations," said Wanda, wickedly.

"Actually, she's been very transparent with me, which I appreciate. It's no good raising my spirits, only to find there's nothing out there. Anyhow, I thought you'd be checking your flight plans for tonight?"

"Forget that — I've just quit the whole Halloween gig. The skies are getting too crowded for my liking. Firstly, the budget airlines filled up any space left by clouds and now, when flying low, I'm buzzed by drones. It's no wonder I fly off the handle at times."

"Has Liz found anything for you?"

"She offered me some cleaning work, but I brushed that off straightaway. I wanna be on T.V. Anyhow, Sienna, I'm surprised things have got so grave for you?"

"Oh, Wanda, don't mention graves. The fallout following that Brexit thingy — I think it's behind the rise in cremations. New retirement flats stacked up in place of once cherished buildings? Tick. Connected millionaires extending their croquet lawns? Tick. Skateboarding parks for budding graffiti artists who've outgrown roller skates? Tick. But you never see a new planning application for a graveyard do you? Honestly, one house I resorted to haunting last Halloween had five urns spread out across the mantelpiece. It resembled a family of Russian dolls that had fallen out."

"What will you do?"

"Well, I'm also quitting Halloween and getting into the media."

"What, T.V. like me?"

"Nope — writing memoirs and articles on behalf of other people," replied Sienna. "If I don't do it now whilst I'm old enough, it'll never come back to haunt me."

As Wanda and Sienna continued chatting about their plans, the job centre door creaked open and in rolled Plumps Pumpkin.

"Hiya Plumps!" said Sienna. "Don't tell me, you're done with Halloween too?"

"Fraid so," replied Plumps. "Us pumpkins have had enough. The government bangs on about the obesity problem, yet no-one thinks of us. All that peer pressure to bulk up and be the biggest. Why, there's even competitions based on your weight and appearance. It's all wrong. And it needs to be stopped. Yes, as of midnight tonight the fire in our belly goes out. The horror of Halloween will be no more. The pumpkins are revolting!"

"Well said!" said Sienna, "But what'll you do instead?"

"Well, I'm here to see what apprenticeship courses are on offer — maybe re-train as a bird feeder. Anything but this — I'll end up going to seed."

"Well, best of luck, Plumps," said Wanda.

As Plumps rolled his way towards Liz's desk, the room plunged into darkness. A darkness blacker than freshly mined coal. The sort of darkness swallowing up the depths of the deepest tunnel.

"Sorry! My bad." said Wanda. "My broomstick fell against the light switch... there we go. All back on."

As Plumps rolled back out of the wastepaper basket he'd inadvertently ended up in, his nerves weren't calmed by an eerie creaking noise encircling the room.

"Sorry!" said Wanda, returning to her seat. "My bad again! My knackered back's playing up. The handle on the cauldron snapped last Halloween and it jarred my body something chronic."

"That's an accident at work," said Sienna. "You should claim for that. Ask Liz, she might have a form you can fill out. Or, more likely these days, several forms designed to take so long you end up not bothering."

"I will, thanks," said Wanda. "And don't worry... I'll just fill them out in spells."

As Wanda made her way to queue up behind Plumps, Ivor Spider crawled under the door.

"Hello, Ivor!" said Sienna. "What brings you here, apart from a surplus of legs?"

"Well, you know I used to drop in at kids Halloween parties. Doing nicely for myself I was... me mates even nick-named me, *The Money Spider*. But new Health & Safety legislation regarding phobias has brought the jam jar down on that one, so to speak. Anorakaphobia I think it's called. I wouldn't mind, but I don't even wear a coat."

"So, what have you got planned?" said Sienna.

"I'm here to gain a new qualification, by signing up for an *Open University* course. I've heard they're web based — which is ideal as I can study from home."

And with that the door whooshed open, scattering Liz's application forms everywhere. As a fortuitous late afternoon mist dispersed, a tall figure cloaked in black emerged into view.

"Dracula?" said Sienna. "At Halloween?"

"Oh, this?" said Arthur Skeleton, taking off his cloak. "It's that Autumn wind... goes right through me these days. But that's actually why I'm here... I'm packing Halloween in. It's got way too commercial. And don't get me started about my lack of presence on *Face-spook*."

"Same here," said Sienna. "I've quit Halloween too."

"Have you, Sienna Ghost?" replied Arthur.

Sienna raised her eyes to the heavens, cursing her parent's lack of forethought. "What will you do now, Arthur... have you put any feelers out?"

"Thinking a complete career change — maybe do some modelling work for the medical profession."

"Well," said Sienna, "that only leaves Bartholomew Bat and his gang flying the flag for Halloween."

"Oh, haven't you heard... he's grounded," said Arthur. "He came in here yesterday seeking a new skills grant to form a night-time air display team with his mates. *'Putting the bat into acrobatic'* he called it."

"Nice."

"However, Liz over there couldn't see the idea taking off, on account of his insistence they'd only perform in the dark, along with taking most of winter and spring off. And, get this, as their only routine would be synchronised hanging upside down off a tree... she accused him of seeking funding for, basically, sleeping on the job."

"No?!" said Sienna, "I bet Bartholomew got in a right flap about that?"

"Sure did, he stormed out like a... oh, you can imagine. Anyhow, he's now suing the job centre for slander. Liz, over there, could be the other side of her desk soon."

"Looks like she already is," said Arthur. "Oh, no, hang on... she's closing up."

As Liz finished collecting up her papers, she noticed no-one was moving.

"Look you lot," said Liz. "It's nearly six o'clock, and in the last two days you've had me covering ageism, the decline of the high street, overcrowded skies, Brexit, obesity, accidents at work claims, health and safety, social media and finally, slander. So, if you don't mind, I've got a party to go to tonight."

And with that, Liz cajoled the motley crew out of the job centre, turned the sign round to *'Closed,'* and locked the door.

"And she thinks we live in a surreal world," said Sienna.

"Well, without us, her Halloween party will be deadly quiet... because Halloween is no more!" said Wanda. "Hey! Why don't you all come back to mine and celebrate as we're not working tonight? I've got into distilling these trendy craft gins of late. This week's one has got just about every herb under the sun in it — well, except garlic, obvs."

And so, following a chorus of approval, Wanda retrieved her broomstick from against the fire exit door, and adjusted the brushes for take-off.

"Sienna, you go ahead and let everybody in whilst I fly round and pick up Bartholomew and his squadron."

Then, as they made to leave, a deathly screech enveloped the job centre car park, setting everyone's senses on edge. Like talons scraping down a chalkboard.

"What the hell is that racket?!" exclaimed Sienna.

"Oh, that'll be the Hound of the Baskerville," replied Plumps. "He's practising for his appearance on tonight's Halloween-themed addition of *X Factor*. Stands a good chance. Maybe we could watch it at Wanda's?"

"Ummm, I think we're better off finding out the result tomorrow, when the tabloids deem it front page news," replied Sienna.

"After the last two days," smiled Plumps, "I've a feeling they'll be cancelled and another motley crew will be front page news tomorrow..."

The Dog on the Train

Heartley Bulldog had caught the 7.43am commuter train into Paddington every morning for the last five years. But how much longer could he bear it?

Same old grey office building.

Same old prospects.

The only thing that changed was the cost of his season ticket.

The train often stopped at a set of signals just outside Barking. The embankment overlooked a small industrial estate, but one unit had always caught his eye, the signage proclaiming... *"Smedgwicks – make a pig of yourself!"* The unit looked pristine, and all the people working there wore smart uniforms of white lab coats and matching hats. The morning summer sun glinted silver shards of sunlight off the modern steel and glass structure.

Then, one day, he saw something that could change everything.

Now they'll see; he's more than just the dog on the train.

When he was a young pup it'd all seemed so exciting, scampering down the platform and hopping on the train to the big City. Feeling proud and happy, picking up his first suit from *Making Strides in the City* — with the trouser seat custom altered to allow his tail to wag free. Something it was doing a lot less nowadays.

His career as a highways designer had taken various twists and turns but he'd reached a crossroads in his life. The last assignment as a cul-de-sac designer looked to have opened all sorts of opportunities — but turned into another dead-end job. On the upside, the pay was ok, allowing him to buy a detached kennel on the desirable side of the park. But Heartley Bulldog wanted a more fulfilling role to sink his teeth into.

Monday 3rd July 2023

"Next stop Barking," informed the Guard, as he checked tickets.

"But I haven't said a word," quipped Heartley, to the familiar delight of the rest of carriage 4B. Well, apart from Forbes-Carruthers, a veteran commuter who'd enjoyed a lengthy and unopposed reign over their first-class carriage. He dispatched a rueful look over the top of his bifocals in Heartley's direction, admonishing the dog's insistence of talking during the journey. Then, neatly folding his newspaper and placing his first-class train pass on top, Forbes-Carruthers left the carriage.

"Be glad to see back of old fart," grumbled the Guard. "Me or me colleagues have suffered bumptious sod nigh on 20 year. Been even worse since his wife passed away couple of year back. Don't get me wrong... terribly sad an' all, but he doesn't have to take it out on us. He told the ticket office he retires next week and, trust me, it'll be first time since Flying Scotsman hit 'undred mile an hour, we've had champagne in't staff canteen. He'll probably be even worse when he ain't got a job to go to. Tickets please fellas... thanks. See you all tomorrow."

"Did you hear that, lads?" said Heartley, "We should do something to commemorate it."

"Yeah," sniggered Colin, "join the Guards in the staff canteen!"

As Forbes-Carruthers pulled back the carriage door and then slammed it shut behind him, carriage 4B obligingly fell silent. Well, almost silent.

"Has the Guard been and checked all the tickets?" enquired Forbes-Carruthers, staring, as he often did, towards Heartley.

"Yes FC, and the winner of the out-of-date buffet car pork pie is seat 57c in cattle class," replied Heartley, to the enjoyment of all in the carriage. Well, apart from Forbes-Carruthers who, although inherently disapproving of Heartley's over familiarity, found the abbreviation added a certain distinction that was rather agreeable.

Wednesday 5th July 2023

"Here, Heartley, old two-names has gone to the toilet — last night's port and stilton must be working its magic. Go on, grab his paper and black out a few boxes on the crossword," encouraged John, both fellow commuter and all-round bad influence.

"No way! His crossword's sacred. But I'll flick through the greyhound racing results. Oooh... no, hang on chaps. The lonely-hearts column looks good today. Here, what about this one...

"Sixty-five-year-old recently retired Deputy Head of Stationery in a very large office. Enjoys collecting cricket scorecards, listening to the lunchtime shipping forecast and evenings in operating a tenth-scale model railway of the Great Western line (1964-68 timetables). Seeks financially secure female companion."

"FC could finally complete one of his crosswords by the time that one gets a reply."

"Or, what about this one... *'Dog seeks rabbit for short term relationship. Must enjoy active outdoor pursuits.'* Whoops! That one's mine..."

As the train's brakes screeched up towards the red signal,

Heartley began folding the paper away exactly how FC did.

And then he saw it!

The job adverts page caught his eye like some sort of calling.

'Smedgwicks Job Vacancy – New Product Taster.'

Now Heartley knew he had to satisfy his curiosity. What went on at Smedgwicks and, more importantly, should he become a part of it?

Thursday 6th July 2023

"Here's one for us to contemplate this morning chaps," offered Heartley, "Can a man with a beard tell a bare-faced lie?"

Forbes-Carruthers put his pen down and raised his paper hoping no one spotted the involuntary smile spreading across his face. Positive emotions still felt disrespectful to Elsie's memory.

"How's the colouring in of the crossword going, FC?" asked Heartley.

"What? Oh... not that it's any of your business dog, but I only have one left. If it were four letters, began with *'c'* and the clue was, *'something dogs chase,'* I would surely seek your wise counsel."

"Ahhh... go on FC. We heard you're leaving us soon; so, you may as well share it with the whole class."

Forbes-Carruthers was forced to admit, the dog had a point. In three decades of trying, he'd never got this close to winning the posh pen crossword prize.

"County pigs used to lying in blankets. Ten letters, beginning with c."

As the carriage fell into silence, Forbes-Carruthers almost

derived as much satisfaction from their ignorance as getting his hands on the prized pen. The pen he'd paid for many times over in trying to complete the darn crossword. After several moments of blissful silence, Forbes-Carruthers suddenly had an inkling.

"Ah! Must be *"chipolatas."* My dear wife always insisted when it came to snoring pigs in blankets, she was an expert. Such a wonderful cook was Elsie."

As his fellow commuters stifled schoolboy sniggers, Forbes-Carruthers momentary joy sank into depths of despair.

"Bloody buffoons! My chipolatas doesn't fit with ten across. They've clearly made a ruddy error."

"Next stop Barking," interrupted the tannoy.

"Oh well chaps, that's me today," said Heartley, "Important meeting. But before I go, FC..."

"What is it now, dog?"

"Cumberland."

"What? What the dickens are you on about?"

"County pigs in blankets, ten letters... Cumberland*!* Both a type of sausage and small..."

"Yes, yes! I get it. Well er... I don't know what to say, er... Heartley Bulldog. That's most kind. Well done, dog. I've solved the crossword at last. Elsie... Elsie would have been so pleased to see this."

"You can still show it off to your work colleagues, FC. Talking of which, FC... may I ask what you do?"

"Did... my dear dog. Did. I'm retiring at the end of next week from my senior position as deputy head of stationery at a very large office. Though why they want to lose a man of my considerable experience I'll never know. What they call efficiency driven management apparently."

Friday 7th July 2023

"Next stop Barking," informed the Guard, as familiar glances awaited Heartley's customary retort.

"Heartley... you alright?" enquired George.

"What?... err, yep. Sorry, George, no time to talk. Mutt on a mission," replied Heartley, reaching under his seat and grabbing his briefcase.

"I'm Barking today," announced Heartley, folding his copy of *Horse & Hound* under his arm. "See you all tomorrow morning. Bonsoir!"

And with that Heartley left the carriage in search of pastures new... a fresh challenge... a new beginning. Or, more specifically, Smedgwicks.

"You've got to love him, haven't you?" smiled George, as all but one of the rest of the carriage nodded.

"Can someone shut the carriage door properly." mumbled Forbes-Carruthers.

"Thirty years in the pork pie industry, lad is telling me you're not here for the part-time Head of Stationery job," said Mr Jenkins, boss of *Sedgwick's Pork Pies,* as Heartley waddled into his office.

"I... er, I mean no. I've only seen the advert for New Product Taster. Not that stationery is my area really," replied Heartley.

"Seems it's no one's ruddy area. Stationery's not the fast-moving career youngsters crave nowadays. And we here at...

why are you sniggering, lad?"

"You said stationery wasn't fast-moving sir... a sort of amusing play on words."

"What? Oh yes... I s'pose it was. Ha ha! Clever old me. Anyway lad, seems everyone only wants to be on ruddy telly these days. All I've been asking for is a hard-working safe pair of hands but, enough of me whinging. Go on then... why should I give you the tasting job?"

"I'm very passionate about my food sir. I've also got experience, having had a part-time job at the village butchers to help pay for my Kennel Club exams. Unfortunately, someone took stock taking too literally and me and the other part-timer, a dachshund, both got the chop. But we both knew the only one who should have had his collar felt."

"Ha! Got the chop... I like it Heartley."

"What? Oh yeah... good spot sir." replied Heartley, thinking to himself Mr Jenkins had missed the better one.

"Well, you come across as both very keen and honest, Heartley, which is more than can be said for most of the rabble that I've seen this week," said Mr Jenkins, warming to the potential new recruit.

"I do like someone with an appetite for work. So, Heartley... Heartley, what is it now?"

"New Product Taster... appetite for the job. Good one sir."

"Oh yes. Ha! Quite the young Bob Monkhouse aren't I, Heartley. D'ya know what lad, I think we're going to enjoy having you around the place. And here's my business card with my contact details; so when Human Resources write to you officially, make sure you send the paperwork back to me, so I can speed everything through. Welcome on-board Heartley!"

“Oh wow! Thank you, sir, — you won’t regret it. Just one question though...”

“There always is, lad. Go on.”

“Do I get my own hat?”

“Of course, Heartley, but... er, it will need a couple of adjustments for your ears.”

“Great! I’ll drop it off with my tailor tomorrow when I pop into town to hand in my notice. My own hat... wow! Thank you, Mr. Jenkins.”

And with that, Heartley proffered his paw and trotted out of Mr Jenkin’s office towards a new beginning, via four spins of giddy happiness in reception’s revolving door. Much to the surprise of an arriving courier.

His happiness continued as Heartley stopped off at *Barks & Spendsless* to splash out on some celebratory posh nosh. Reaching into his waistcoat pocket for his wallet he inadvertently pulled out Mr Jenkin’s business card and, staring at it, wondered if he’d ever be important enough to have his own card. And then he had a brilliant idea. Smiling to himself, he paid for his Bonios and bottle of Evian sparking water before trotting off home to implement his cunning plan.

Friday 14th July 2023

As carriage 4B spilled out on to the terminus platform, Forbes Carruthers doffed his trilby to his now ex-fellow commuters, and trudged towards the escalator. Whilst he’d never describe them as friends, they’d helped fill the emptiness of the last couple of years.

Heartley said goodbye to his train chums and scampered off after Forbes-Carruthers.

"Got time for a quick coffee, FC?"

"What? Er... hardly, I'll be late for work, dog. Only late once in 30 years of commuting. A blasted baboon escaped from a zoo in '97 and wouldn't climb down from the signal gantry until some sort of banana ransom was paid. Selfish idiot."

"C'mon FC, it's your last day... what's the worst they can do? Go on, just a few minutes of your time. Pretty please!"

"Ahhh... well, if you insist dog," sighed FC. "I can get a taxi afterwards I suppose. Won't be able to put it on expenses mind. Just make it quick."

"Great! Walk this way FC," encouraged Heartley, with his best waddle heading off towards the *Costa-Lotta* coffee kiosk. Forbes-Carruthers followed, pausing momentarily to dab his eyes with a silk handkerchief. He'd miss the reassuring comfort of the weekly work routine. But, more worryingly, he was going to miss the ruddy dog.

"What's this?" asked Forbes-Carruthers, as Heartley slid Mr Jenkins business card across the table.

"He's my new boss and I know he's looking for a Head of Stationery. And the hours are negotiable — ideal for a Captain of Industry easing his way into retirement. Plus, it's half the travelling time — so you'll still be our Head of Commuter Club, just in a bite-size portion."

"Well... er, thank you... Heartley. It's awfully sweet of you thinking of me, but... but I'll be fine. There's... there's the garden to attend to for one thing. It's all got a bit overgrown since... well, you know. And I'll also have time to take up a hobby, like... er... painting landscapes maybe."

"Big mistake, FC. I'm telling you; you'll miss the structure of a daily routine and the buzz from an office of colleagues. You can't sit around all day playing trains and listening to the shipping forecast."

"What!" said Forbes Carruthers, jolting up from staring down at his shoes. "How did you know about that?"

"I'm more than just *The Dog on the Train*," winked Heartley. "At least think about it eh?"

And with that Heartley snapped shut his briefcase, sprang off his stool and put a paw round Forbes-Carruthers' shoulders.

"It's been great getting to know you, FC. I guess what we had in common was we were both a bit different to the others, eh?"

"Umm, yes... maybe. Er... have you... have you time for a top up, Heartley?"

"Sorry, FC, got a meeting with HR at 10am; it's also my last day today. I start as New Product Taster at Smedgwicks next week, but..." smiled Heartley opening his Fidofax, "here's a pen, well biro, to remember me by when you're colouring in the crossword."

Waving back at Heartley's retreating figure, Forbes-Carruthers knew he'd cherish the pen. Even it did have *Barclays Bank* written down the side. Then, looking at the business card lying in front of him, he smiled at the thought of what Elsie would say of his intention to take up gardening. Or painting for that matter.

And it dawned on him how to make Elsie proud.

Wednesday 19th July 2023

"I'm glad you made contact, Mr Forbes-Carruthers; with your wealth of experience you're exactly what we need here at Smedgwicks. Any questions?"

"Just one, please."

"Go on..." smiled Mr Jenkins.

"My business card will still say *'Head'* of stationery, notwithstanding the flexible hours we've agreed?"

"Certainly and, as I've had a very good run at recruiting recently, it will be in bold. Embossed. Now, if you'd just fill in the standard HR form, you know — contact numbers, bank account details, agency used for the darn commission purposes..."

"There's no agency involved, Mr. Jenkins. Your New Product Taster kindly passed on your details but, for interview integrity, I've implied otherwise. I trust you both understand and forgive my duplicity."

"What! Heartley Bulldog? Well, I never. Better put some overtime his way as a thank you. Welcome on-board Mr Forbes-Carruthers."

"Oh, please... call me FC."

Friday 4th August 2023

"Greetings FC!" barked Heartley Bulldog, waddling up to the park bench that was their regular lunchtime meeting place since becoming work colleagues.

"Afternoon, Heartley, I've reserved your usual seat old chap."

“Cheers FC. So, what are we debating today... the effect of Brexit on the pork pie sector, how best to nudge the canteen’s snack dispenser without setting the alarm off...”

“Well, er... actually Heartley I was, umm... hoping to ask your advice on something that’s been troubling me.”

“Fire away, FC... like Bugs Bunny, I’m all ears.”

“Er, yes... quite. May I start by asking if you’re currently stepping out with anyone?”

“Nah... recently split up with a French poodle I’d been sniffing around with for a couple of years.”

“Must have been difficult for you?”

“Not really... it was doing me in how long it took her to get ready. I tell you, by the time she finished, her hair had more bunches than a banana plantation. Glad to see the back of her, as it were. Anyhow, let’s talk about something else — like whether Chelsea should play a flat back four, or go with three at the back and an extra man in midfield.”

“Er... well, actually old chap I couldn’t care less if Chelsea played all fifteen or, however many of them there are, at the back, front or down the sides. No, I seek your counsel on a rather delicate personal matter.”

Heartley put his lunch box down on the bench and cocked his head to one side.

“I’m taking a lady called Anne out to lunch at the weekend...”

“Whoa! Way to go, Casanova!” said Heartley, offering an unreciprocated high-five.

“Now Heartley, Heartley... please don’t get carried away. But... but I’d appreciate some advice as to... oh, sorry... excuse me Heartley, that's my phone vibrating. This could be the lady in question — do you mind awfully if I take it?"

"Fire away, FC — I'm just grateful it was your phone and not one of our pork pies escaping." And with that Heartley started drawing a moustache on the cover dog of his *Horse and Hound,* as FC paced round the bench with his hand cupped over the mouthpiece.

"Let me just write that down, Anne... 37 Seawater Avenue, on the left just after the parade of shops. Lovely, I look forward to picking you up on Saturday, half past twelve. Good day, Anne."

"Nice posh pen, FC, is it new?"

"As a matter of fact it is, Heartley," smiled Forbes-Carruthers, "finally arrived in the post this morning. Now, where was I...?"

"Romeo was planning to take Juliet out."

"Ah yes. Thank you, Heartley... very droll. No, what I was about to ask was that I'd, err, I'd appreciate any advice you're able to impart regarding managing the occasion. It's been a while since... well, you know."

"Standard stuff really, FC. Hold the restaurant door open, insist on paying at least your half of the bill, listen and talk in equal measure and, most importantly, try not to talk about Elsie too much. Now, obviously I never met Elsie but, if she loved you anywhere near as much as you did, and always will, love her, I'm sure she'd want you to find happiness again. And Anne won't want to dilute your lovely memories of Elsie; but she may be able to help you create new ones together."

"Umm... thanks Heartley, that's... that's truly helped put things into perspective. I wasn't sure you'd be the right one to turn to for such advice but, I don't have anyone else I trust. Do you know what Heartley?"

"What, FC?"

"You're so much more than just The Dog on the Train."

The Ripple Effect

"Either smuggle the bulldog onto an inflatable in the Lido or, you're dressing as Wonder Woman for the whole weekend. Stag weekend rule number one."

"I still think you should've stuck him in kennels, Tom, but go on, hand me your jacket."

"My jacket?"

"Your dog, your jacket. Stag weekend rule number two."

"Don't forget two sets of armbands for him! And mobile phone video required as proof."

***

"That's quick... what happened?"

"Got kicked out. Fido was caught peeing in the pool."

"Bit harsh... I thought kids did that anyway."

"He was on their diving board at the time!"

PETER LUCAS

Peter lives in the New Forest. He learned to write very late and never entirely learned to spell. His childhood was entirely without television. Yet he grew up in a house of books.

He was blessed with a magnificent Grandfather, custodian of ancient family stories, who also read to him the best books in the English language. The old man gave him a love of language and story.

His writing is deeply rooted in the natural world and the land of Britain. Delve into it. You may uncover a touch of magic and a little of the wisdom of working people, from time out of mind.

Pamper Day

Pamper day.
Dolly, Marge and May.

Not looking your best.
My gloves are on.
Running away won't help.
Come here.
I see the problem.

What's this?
Looks painful.
Won't fix itself.
You have to trust me.

Don't get flustered.
Just a pair of scissors.
Don't struggle.
Your sisters are watching.
Awaiting their turn.

I'm holding you.

Water helps.
There you are, nice and warm.
Bubbles and baby shampoo.
I'll be gentle.

Don't be embarrassed.
Relax.
It's coming away quite easily.
Sorry I ruffled your feathers.

Nearly finished.
A quick blow dry.
Off you go.
Back to the Chicken Coop.

The Last Stop Shop

I'm much too old for this. I must look a sight, running down the road at my age. Shambling really, but the way the breath is rasping in my throat, it does feel like running. Look at that sky, it's getting blacker by the minute. Oh, here it comes. Stair rods smacking down on the pavement and bouncing back up again. I'm getting soaked twice, above and below. I should be used to it by now, after all I've lived in the Pennines all my life.

At last, I reach the stop. Well, they don't build bus shelters like they used to. I can remember when they had at least three sides and seats. This one's got one side and a bit of a roof that keeps about half the rain off. That narrow shelf of hard blue plastic, along the back, is just something to lean on. I'm not as tall as some people, so as I lean, it digs into my spine. Growing old isn't much fun.

Now where is my shopping list? I can see it now on the kitchen table. The question is, did I pick it up? Still, here's the bus. A smart step back and I'm avoiding the muddy wave of water squeezed out of the gutter onto the pavement by the wheels.

I drop my walking stick as I fumble for my bus pass.

"Morning Miss." I glance up at him. He smiles back. "Take your time Miss." The bus stays where it is, while I get a peep from the scanner and make my way up the aisle. "Thanks Joe," I say, as I sink gratefully into my seat. The engine roars and we speed down Topley Pike Hill to join the main road. Sitting back, I watch the trees flash by and wonder where all the time has gone. Despite the rain I see the shops and houses bathed in the sunshine of those endless summers of long ago. Under a blue sky, framed by the green wooded hills that surround the town.

Only on the war memorial does the rain still pitilessly pour down. Just like every week, my eyes start to smart and I look away. Some memories are just too painful.

Still, I remember driver Joe; he was little Joe then. How long must it be? 20 years if it's a day. Being remembered keeps you going, so they say. Looking back is all I do these days. Oh, and I do remember Joe. A painfully shy five-year-old, holding tightly to his mum's hand, peeping round her back and refusing to meet my eye. As they both come in hesitantly, almost apologetically, into my classroom at Hardwick Square school, all those years ago. Seems like only yesterday.

My body moves with the movement of the bus. My mind slips back again. I've had a very full life. Highs and lows. The lowest part sits on my old mum's Welsh dresser. Wherever I go, it goes. A photograph in a small silver frame. He's smiling just for me. Proud in his blue uniform and white cap with its red ribbon. So pleased that I was there at his passing out parade.

Just a year later I remember feeling unaccountably low, that June of 1982. It puzzled me because I had been very happy, having everything to wish for and look forward to. My world came to an end on one dark night, half a world away at a place I'd never heard of – Two Sisters ridge, near Port Stanley, on the Falkland Islands. I couldn't grieve openly for him because our love was our secret. Though inside I was empty.

Meeting Jane was the turning point for me in some kind of return to happier times. I'd moved schools in 1983, wanting to put some distance between me and my sorrow. Older than me, she was already teaching at the school and helped me settle in. We soon became great friends. A year or so later we became much more to each other.

Jane had been married and had twin six-year-old girls. Though the marriage hadn't worked out and she was a single mum. We had to be discreet. At that time curious people were quick to talk and to judge. Jane took a teaching job on the other side of the county. My life had turned itself around. I had a ready-made family who loved me and a job I adored. The twins left home and made lives and families of their own. We made the most of the grandchildren.

Retirement came and I welcomed it; time for me, time for us. And there was time, but not enough of it. Jane put a brave face on illness. We made the most of the time that we had together. Now I'm on my own. No need for a house anymore. I live in a small flat just off Valley Road.

In the old days I was very organised, making lists and keeping tabs on things, what I did and where. "To do" lists were all important. There were monthly shops and weekly top ups. Now I have time on my hands, more than I know what to do with. So shopping is no longer a planned operation to feed the family. It is, rather, an excuse, nay necessity, to get out of the flat. So going shopping is an outing for me. Something I look forward to.

So that's why I'm on this bus to the supermarket.

'Ding.' The stop bell rouses me as we arrive.

"Bye Joe."

"Bye Miss."

Making sure I have my walking stick, bags and the all-important bus pass, I get off the bus and make my way across the car park, head down against the east wind.

I hear the metallic clash of massed shopping trolleys on the move. It brings my head up and I am rewarded with a smile as wide as the sky. "Are you off shopping Miss?" roars Peter. A slow learner is Peter. It's taken him a long time to find his niche. He lives in the independent living project on Holker Road. He does a fine job, has a heart of gold and even has a girlfriend. I'm very proud of him. He shouts something as I step inside the store. I stop and cup my hand to my ear. He speaks again. "Hey

Miss, we've got a new manager we have..." He says something else, but I don't catch it. The automatic door slides between us. I smile and wave. He smiles and waves back.

Mary is on the first checkout. Looking up, she manages to smile and wave, without pausing her speed scanning. I'm looking forward to having a chat with her. I'm very keen to catch up with the lives of her young family.

I walk up and down the aisles getting this and that, most of which I don't really need. I'm having precious snatches of conversation with Jill (fresh produce), Arthur (bakery), Kim (hot chicken), Kelly (pharmacy), Tony (electrical), and Wayne (grocery). I know everyone who works here, and they know me. In the past I've taught them to read, settled arguments, given encouragement, set boundaries, seen them grow and move on. I've even been to several weddings, two christenings and sadly one funeral. They are all my children. The ones I never had, and they have become the sinews of my life. Getting more and more important as I get older.

I'm in household goods when I catch sight of him. A tall figure in a blue pinstripe suit. Must be the new manager. I feel faint, my heart all of a flutter. Maybe I've been walking too fast. An unaccountable dread has risen within me. What's the matter with me? He turns, and his eyes light with recognition. He stares at me for a long moment. I stand helpless, rooted to the spot. There is no warmth or apology in those eyes, just a steely coldness. It takes me a while to place him. I find that I am shivering as realisation dawns. It is Raymond. After all these years. School bully and terror of the younger children. Biter, arm twister, kicker, puller of hair, and thief. He and I have had more run-ins than I can remember.

I move on. Later I have my chat with Mary at checkout number one and, warmed by it, I go out to the bus stop. I feel a hard hand, heavy on my shoulder. The uniformed security man looms over me. My heart thumps.

Later, in the manager's office, my shopping is spread out upon the desk. Raymond Hill gives me a cold smile heavy with satisfaction. Between his thumb and forefinger, he holds a ladies compact. I've never seen it before. Not that it matters now. There is a two-way mirror running the full length of the far wall. In it I see the faces of the children that I have lost, suffused with shock and incredulity. Now I am truly alone.

The Blackbird

Looking out of my window.

The sky casts a warm red glow in the west. Shadows are lengthening, though there is still enough light to look out into the garden, on this New Forest summer's evening.

***

Our own horizon has shrunk; we are locked down for most of our day, every day. Sometimes we look back wistfully to a sparkling spring, more than a year ago. The seeking out of the quiet green places between the Loire and the Sierra Tramuntana, seem like a dream now.

We take our daily Forest walk, just as the sun rises. Our way is over open heath and into the greenwood under an unblemished sky, amid birdsong and glimpses of deer. On our return, we are in a closed and different world, wrapped around by our garden hedge.

***

There he is again and what a sight he is. Clumsily hopping about in the branches, sometimes frantically fluttering his wings to get a balance. His feathers stick out in all directions; he is constantly trying to put them back in order. It has been like this for weeks now.

Possibly, he has had a brush with a car. Or fallen between the paws of that longhaired Persian feline, murderer and trespasser. A cold-hearted killer who, having a taste for young birds, first disables and then plays with them. He makes a wary entry into the garden, whenever he gets the chance. Leaving behind the tortured bodies of Dunnock, Sparrow, Chaffinch and Tit. Even our favourite Robin.

***

It seems that whatever happened to him, our young Blackbird barely escaped with his life. Mind you that was some time ago; the down and lost feathers have blown away now.

***

Somehow, our Blackbird's fate has become important to us. We look back to when he first came to our hedge. Bright of eye, yellow of beak, smooth of feather and sleek of body. He steadfastly defended his part of the hedge against all comers, chasing away rivals with a flourish. Singing his heart out, whenever the beautiful, brown young female flew up and on to the hedge, to look him over.

My mind flies back 60 years, to another, different world. To my grandparents' house, looking out on their garden in spring. Full of birds feeding on scattered seed and hanging coconut shells. I hear it all still.

"May! May, look at this, Blackie's come."

Always the same answer.

"Well stir yourself Will, fill up the feeders. I'll put the kettle on."

"Right, you are May."

The small boy, tucking into his bacon and eggs at the table, raises his eyes to the ceiling, before returning to the task before him. There was always food at grandma's house, but you had to eat everything on your plate.

***

So now we watch our Blackbird carefully. Something is wrong. It is not just the clumsiness, the falling and the flapping. He looks vacant and unaware. The great black corvids: Magpies, Crows and Rooks, fly close to him, he doesn't seem to notice. He still sticks to his post on the hedge, but seems not to know why he is there.

The she bird stops coming. She has a mate, nest, eggs and a busy life elsewhere.

"I don't think he's eating."

***

We make a plan. It is about making contact. Tempting him with different kinds of food. He's not having any. You can get as close as you like. He only moves at the last moment and then just a little way up the hedge. We keep trying. We accompany our efforts with what we imagine is encouraging bird sounds. I put my tongue against my front teeth. Sucking in air, we make tch, tch, tch sounds in bands of three. He puts his head on one side as if totally puzzled. It seems we cannot speak Blackbird.

Still, we try out bits from the table, mixed grain, porridge oats, sunflower hearts, Niger seeds, oh hang the expense. Even those horrible mealworms.

Sadly, we watch the long-eared field mouse steal food from under his beak. This is hanging open now. He is listless, uninterested in anything around him. It seems that there is no way back for him.

***

It is morning and pink in the East, a new day. We try again, making 'come and get it' noises, in Blackbird. Much too early to be awake, either for us, or for him. "Bugger, I've only got those awful mealworms."

We scatter them near him. As usual, his head goes on one side and we return indoors.

We get a cup of tea. Looking out of the window, we notice a black shape moving below the hedge.

"It's the mealworms. He's eating them."

"God bless mealworms."

***

Update

Things have been improving for our Blackbird, especially over the last few days. He's still not quite where he was when he first came to us. We continue to hope that he will survive. Though now, he hoovers up mealworms with enthusiasm.

Today he has been joined by an unattached female. Fingers crossed there may yet be a part two to this story.

Pinky and the Child

The Characters

A beautiful shepherdess.

A large and venerable cat.

A very small boy.

The Action

All takes place in a council house. Deep in the early 1950s. On the edge of a once well-to-do town in the north of England, now a little threadbare, its finest buildings showing their age.

Underneath the sink in the back kitchen, the curtain twitched. Within that small space, sitting companionably side-by-side were a large cat and the child. Strictly speaking this was Pinky's place. Though as he had finished both milk and cat food, he didn't seem to mind. Pinky, named for his pink nose, was a cat, and a big cat at that. He had great yellow eyes like marbles, that shone in the dark. A bright white front, with paws to match. His back was silver. His tail, alternately banded in black, silver and white, was magnificent. On the end of it was a great black plume, which when erect stood twice the height of the child.

Everyone was at work and Grandma was in the garden. Pinky and the child had the house to themselves.

The front room, like the front garden, was beautifully kept. A place for the rare and the precious. It was for important visitors and only used by the family on Sundays, high days and holidays. The door was seldom opened during the week. Unaccountably it stood ajar on that Monday morning. Marvelling at the unexpected opportunity, the child slipped in.

"This is the front room."

So said the child, spreading his hands in a wide circle. The cat knew what it was, but forbore to comment. Soon they were both inside. The pair passed the secretaire, its light oak polished to a deep shine. The child wouldn't have been able to reach high enough to touch the key, let alone turn it.

In any case he was staring lovingly toward the windowsill. Their eyes met. The figure that looked back at him had a translucent white face, blue eyes and golden hair. In her right hand she held a shepherd's crook. On seeing the boy, she demurely cast down her bright blue eyes. Looking at the pair of little lambs at her feet, she wore a secret smile. The child drank in this vision of loveliness and whispered confidentially to the cat. Saying softly,

"I'm going to marry her when I grow up."

Pinky decided that it was time to show an interest and get a closer look. He leapt lightly up onto the windowsill and padded along its edge, to inspect the lovely little figure. Purring, he turned around, his big front paws marking time and kneading the shiny surface. Overcome by her beauty, he raised his tail in salute.

Somehow the lovely shepherdess hooked herself onto his magnificent black plume. She rose gracefully into the air, teetering momentarily on the sill. Looking reproachfully at the child, and the cat, she stepped out into space. There followed a delicate tinkling of music, as she hit the floor.

Pinky and the child stared down at her brokenness. It was time to go.

Back under the sink, the child drew the curtains and, moments later, the cat squeezed in beside him. The pair looked at each other. The child whispered accusingly.

"You killded her."

His lower lip thrust out, his eyes screwed up tight, trying to be brave. He was already on the edge of tears.

Pinky did what cats do when overcome by shame and embarrassment. Not looking at the child, he turned himself away, his nose up against the gas meter, and began to wash.

The child pressed his face into the furrowed whitewash of the opposite wall. A solitary tear stole slowly down his cheek. In that quiet space beneath the sink, all was silent misery.

Epitaph for a Generation

They ......

Kept calm and carried on

Lent a hand

Made do and mended

Stood their corner

They ......

Waved them goodbye

Dug for victory

Waited their turn

Stood in the queue

They .....

Kept their pecker up

Did their bit

Soldiered on

Stood fast

They ......

Cheered up

Put their shoulders to the wheel

Saw it all come out in the wash

Stood up and were counted

They ……

Kept smiling through

Made the long way to Tipperary

Laughed, loved and cried

They ……

Are just a memory

We will remember them

We'll meet again

The Blighty One

Bill had a sense of unreality; all was black and black was all. After an age, he began to see something in the shadows. Gradually he perceived that he was in a dense foggy night, clouded out, no moon or stars. It carried with it a sort of distant echoing silence. He realised with a shock that he couldn't feel anything. He was confined to the barracks inside his head.

His inner voice woke up jittery and disorientated. It was running about all over the place, yesterday, today, things that happened years ago.

Christ, that shelling must have been a heavy one. There'd been the usual mind-numbing terror. While cowering in the dugout. Bill struggled to remember. What had the Old Man said? The Old Man; nobody dared to call him Old Man to his face. Though he was the Old Man. Funny bloody war.

The next artillery barrage had been unfamiliar. They'd known it was coming. Strange and frightening. Mustn't show that you are scared. Don't let the side down. Crack a joke. Light a fag.

Stand to, had been two hours old. Everyone in fighting kit, all present and correct. Yesterday Lieutenant Smythe had put Private Isaacs on a charge, for a having a dirty mess tin. For God's sake, in all this bloody mud and mayhem, a dirty mess tin?

Isaacs had been out half the night in no man's land, helping to recover wounded. He'd tried to explain. The lieutenant didn't do explanations. Fresh out from England he wanted to impress the captain and above all – get a medal. The men were very wary about the lieutenant. Chasing medals was the kind of blood sport that they wanted no part in.

It was starting to come back to him now. He'd been standing in the bottom of the trench. Just below the firing step, bayonet fixed, Lee Enfield at his shoulder, eyes glued to the parapet. Far out across no man's land, there was a distant, earth-shaking rumble. Getting louder, getting closer. He'd felt sweat running down the back of his neck from beneath his tin hat. His heart pounding.

The Old Man speaking in his ear.

"Don't worry lad, it's a creeping barrage. It won't get to us for another five minutes. Just before it does you'll all be stood down, in the bottom of the trench while it passes."

"Yes Sarge." Sharp clap on his left shoulder before the Old Man moved on. Threading his way, on the duck boards, along the trench through the company files.

Bill, unconscious again, found himself thinking about the Old Man. How old was the Sergeant? Well, he must be 25? That was it, the Old Man was 25 years old. Bill's own age was 17. He'd been at this caper for nearly two years now.

At first it had felt like being a spy, straight out of the boy's own paper, keeping a secret, out on a mission. That was before he got to France, at Etaples waiting to go up the line. Then it dawned on him, everyone lied about their age.

"Doing your bit," whispered the inner voice.

He'd been working at Harper's stores before the war. His job delivering groceries, by horse and trap, to the big houses of the quality. They'd often send him back again with a flea in his ear, if it wasn't absolutely right. Or they'd decided they didn't want it. Wanted something else. Either way it meant he'd have to deliver again alongside all his other work, by the end of the day, often in the dark. Extra hours unpaid. Still, he loved working with the horses. Although he'd ached for something more.

Then it happened. Somebody shot someone in Sarajevo, and the world changed.

None of the village lads was going to be left out. En masse, they'd marched on Shrewsbury, one bright July morning. Taking the King's shilling at Copthorne Barracks and joining the KSLI (Kings Shropshire light infantry). It would be a great adventure and they could not miss it. Everyone wanted to be in it. Anyway, it would all be over by Christmas. That was then, 1914. This was now, 1916. No end in sight.

A voice came to him, hard to make out, distant and muffled, as from the other end of a long tunnel. He willed himself to be able to peer down it. Saw nothing. Then the voice came again. This time he heard it.

"Bill, are you there lad?"

He tried to speak; he felt his lips moving sluggishly. His throat impossibly dry. There was a weight across his face. He could hardly breathe.

His inner voice tried to make sense of it.

"Some swine's sitting on my face. Hey, play the game, let me up."

Then the taste of warm salty liquid was in this mouth.

***

It had been a brief moment of outside awareness. Now Bill drifted back into unconsciousness and the nightmare in his head. He was vaguely aware that oblivion might be safer.

"Oh God. I'm going to die. To die. Why ever did I join up?"

At last, his inner voice woke up.

"Your country needed you. All the boys from the village went. Besides, you were scared."

"I wasn't scared. I WAS NOT SCARED."

"Oh yes you were. You were terrified of getting a white feather."

Another memory stole its way into Bill's head. His mind going back to a week or so before he and the other village lads joined up.

It was a Saturday, market day in Shrewsbury. Amazingly, old Harper, from the stores, had given him the day off. He'd have to make it up of course. But on the day, it was bliss.

He'd arrived in the sunshine of a summer morning, having got a lift high up on the village blacksmith's substantial wagon. He'd been able to take with him a range of soft fruits, mushrooms, and flowers. Taken from the garden and gleaned from the surrounding countryside. Together with jars of home-made pickles and jams. Even some eggs from Mum's small flock. The crowning glory was six brace of rabbits, table ready. Skinned, gutted, and cleaned. Mum, Lily and Sissy had been up half the night preparing and packing.

Having paid sixpence for the stone market table, he was able to clear his stock in a couple of hours. True, the last jars of piccalilli had gone for half price. Yet he found himself the richer by a red-and-white oxo tin full of copper and a little silver. Farthings, halfpennies, pennies, threepenny bits, sixpences, and even a few shillings. Spreading this fortune upon the table he counted it. It was more than enough.

A smile on his face, he moved on to do some marketing of his own. Pleased that he, his Mum and sisters would eat better this week than last.

Now with two willow baskets in his hands and a pack on his back, he was struggling down the steps from the market. Weighed down with everything Mum had told him to get. Tea, sugar, flour, lard, bacon and salt. Even a link of sausages. Brasso, beeswax polish, carbolic soap, matches, knitting wool and sewing thread. A sack of shallots for pickling. One of carrots. (Carrots didn't grow well in the heavy clay soils around the village.) Carrots were a treat. Best of all there were two thick cakes of chocolate, in his inside pocket, to be savoured and shared.

Bill wasn't the only one making his way out. There was a good-natured, though determined, phalanx of early shoppers, pushing down behind him. Eager to be away. While an equally determined crowd, of all shapes and sizes of humanity, was trying to force its way up and into the market hall.

A pretty girl pushed past him, all ripe corn yellow hair and blue ribbons. Her bright blue eyes smiled at him. Stopping for a moment she placed a hand on his arm and seemed to be wanting to press something soft into his hand. He was transfixed. Abruptly, she was jolted from behind and almost fell. Bill dropped his bags and made to catch her. There was a tall, sharp-featured, hard-faced, older girl behind her. Her voice harsh by Bill's ear.

"Not him. Too young," she snorted.

The tall girl had the face of a hunter. She pointed down into the square. She had sniffed out her quarry.

"There's the mark. Him by the lamp post."

Bill, still struggling with his bags, followed her gaze. He caught sight of a young man in his 20s, in an ill-fitting shabby suit. Even at this distance Bill could see that his arms were too long for his jacket. Must be a clerk, he thought.

By now the girls were pushing their way swiftly down the steps, men and boys touching their caps and letting them through. They closed their ranks as Bill tried to follow. Some minutes later, it was a relief to him to reach the bottom of the steps and put down his burdens at the edge of the pavement. He stood catching his breath and looked out across the square.

Both girls were up close to the young man. Bill caught the sound of laughter. Smiling, the young clerk seemed to be enjoying the attention. The younger, yellow-haired girl was gazing up at him, smiling. He was smiling down at her.

The older girl took his hand and pressed something into it. He looked down, as both girls skipped away, into the crowd. Puzzled, the young man stared at the white feather in his fingers.

The young clerk's face went from joyfully flushed to a deathly white pallor. His head jerked up, moving from side to side, as he looked about him. The head fell back down in anguish as he realised that everyone had seen. Bill saw fear, anger and shame cross his features by turns. The young clerk put the feather in his pocket, as though to hide it. Turning away from Bill's stare. He walked quickly away. As he rounded the corner he began to run.

Bill turned back to his bags and began to stumble across the square. He was longer joyous, flushed with the success of his trading and shopping. Of all that he had to take home to his mother and sisters.

Unaccountably he felt sick. A slow understanding dawned. Somehow, he had caught part of the young clerk's anguish. His shame, panic and despair. Above all, Bill felt empty and tired and a great want to be home again.

***

"Mother. What about mum? How will she look after Cissy and Lily?"

"She's been a widow these 10 years. Widows know how to cope. Besides, Cissy and Lily will muck in and make it work. They've grown up a lot since you left."

"Oh God."

The inner voice was getting angry now.

"Stop snivelling. Women have been coping since Adam was a lad, while men go off and do stupid things. They'll survive and make a good life for themselves. You won't be missed."

"So I am going to die."

"Not that again. Can you hear anything."

"No I can't, I'm ......"

"Hearing is the last sense to go. So try harder."

Bill tried harder and at last it came to him, like a whisper from a long way off.

"Bill. Bill. Are you there Bill?"

The voice again? Who was that? Reuben, it was Rubi. Managing a gurgling groan, he found that there was still the taste of blood in this mouth. He was even able to spit some of it out. Yet to his joy there was no longer a crushing weight upon his chest. Hands were delving down to get him, pulling and scraping at him. He had a glimpse of a brawny arm, freckled with red hairs. Patrick, Pado. He felt himself being lifted. His mates were with him.

He was back. Now being dragged along the bottom of the trench, the duck boards scraping at his back. Where had his tunic gone? At first it was strangely quiet, just a sense of being moved. Seeing the boots, legs and bodies of men trying to make themselves small, heads pushed into the side of the trench. Then the womff of the shockwave, a bursting shell, close and reaching down for him. The air above shrieking with explosions, thick with flying debris, smoke and the cries of men.

Now in the dark. They'd got him down into the dugout. On a bunk no less. A paraffin lamp, set on a wooden ammunition box, seemed to light itself. It cast a pool of yellow light about.

At its edge he could make out two anxious faces looking down at him. Bill tried to smile. Then a searing pain burned through his body; it took over his entirety. He felt himself begin to shake uncontrollably. Such was his agony that he welcomed the blackness that came over him.

Bill found that he was looking down into the yellow light around the bunk. Two men were working feverishly, bent over the slightly-built figure that lay upon it. It was naked and white for the most part. Blood pumping furiously from just above the knee. Curiously detached, Bill looked down at what they were doing. He saw them desperately tightening an army belt around the lower left thigh. There was a sense of relief as the fountain of blood sank to a trickle and stopped.

JULIA PEERS

Julia Peers moved to the Isle of Wight six years ago with her husband and two cats. She spent 35 years working in the NHS as a specialist nurse in a variety of roles in many locations in the UK and Germany. Working on the front-line in diverse areas has informed and influenced her short stories and flash fiction. This, coupled with her unique style and satirical flare adds a comedic dimension to her writing.

She loved writing fiction from an early age and since leaving work has been part of a tutor-led creative writing group facilitated by Brockenhurst College. Developing relationships with other writers in a supportive environment has enabled her to develop her creative passion.

Her writing often reflects her experiences in the NHS where she captures the complexities of the "human condition" through dialogue and characterisation. The themes she writes about include the 1970s and 80s, mental health issues and crime.

She read her work to an audience at The Winchester Writers Festival in 2016 and gained positive feed-back. She is working on two novels at present, a gothic satire and a crime thriller set in an asylum.

All in the Mind?

Please be aware that this short story contains content of a sensitive nature relating to mental illness.

"How now my good woman? Thou hast the beauty of all women and I am blessed to make your acquaintance. I am the Duke of Sherringale and I wish to purchase a ticket for the gallery."

The Duke took a deep bow, doffing his black felt hat adorned with plumed feathers of red and gold.

Belinda stood, looked over the counter and waved him on. "There's only thirty minutes before we close so in you go, no charge."

"I am indebted to you fair lady and I thank you from the very depths of my heart." He turned on his heel, revealing the sapphire blue lining of his velvet cape and the steely shine of buckled shoes which glinted under the artificial light. Taking his ebony cane, he galloped up the steps two at a time with a flourish, removing his hat to an assembled party of tourists, the scars on his wrist concealed by a white bandage.

"Tanya did you see him? Who the hell does he think he is?"

Tanya grinned at her colleague whilst filling the shelves with multi-coloured rock and postcards of Rococo art, the drumming heartbeat of the Midsummer Parade audible through the window.

"He must be part of the Pageant or some kind of Elizabethan re-enactment perhaps. Probably only came in to use the loo. He did look a bugger though; I'll grant you that. Allow me to carry your tray of sweet meats oh fair and wondrous maiden." She giggled as they bowed in turn at each other.

The Duke of Sherringale walked into the vast gallery at the top of the stairs. He stared at the expansive vaulted ceiling bedecked with gold leaf detail. The intricate ceiling and cornicing adorned with carvings of flowers and birds made him gasp for breath. He sighed, drawn to the exquisite stained-glass window stretching from floor to ceiling, the panoply of colours creating vibrant images on the parquet floor.

"Here you all are my beauties," he crooned, pointing with his cane at the portraits hanging on the walls.

He clapped at the witches. "Pray tell me why you have those naked babies in a basket and an owl on your head?" Their eyes moved in unison, staring at him, toothless smiles gurning.

"You have interrupted the witches Sabbath and you will be punished."

He sprang back with alarm, turned to the gilt-framed picture opposite, and watched as the two men eating soup raised their fists at him. The syndics of the clothmakers guild peered at him clothed in black capes. They began to talk, their voices increasing in pace and volume.

A group of scholars from the 16th Century raised their faces with menacing stares.

"Stop glaring at me, there's nothing to see."

He straightened his body, moved with purpose towards them banging the cane on the canvas. To his horror their faces melted, revealing bony protuberances. Hair and skin slowly slid from their heads creating a waxy puddle which smelt of death and decay. He turned to the portrait above the fireplace and saw the image of a baby swaddled in embroidered satin dissolve into the fabric. The shape of the baby, a rotting pile of blood and sinew. The gallery was alive with a cacophony of sounds. Shrieks from the witches, the unremitting wail of children flayed by men in cloaks and the relentless banging of a gong calling them all to order.

"Stop it! Stop it! SILENCE! I can't bear it."

From the corner of the gallery an elephant trumpeted, and a fold of Highland cattle prepared to charge. The head of a rhinoceros snorted pungent liquid onto his shoes. He leapt towards the window in desperation, jumping from foot to foot before discovering that the sticky rancid substance had disappeared.

As the sounds increased, he sank to his knees shaking. With hands clamped to his ears he screamed.

"STOP NOW. NO MORE. BE SILENT."

A door opened and a uniformed man stepped into the gallery. "Hey mate, are you okay? We're closing in five minutes."

The Duke turned, staring at the man's face, raising his cane.

"Tell them to stop. The witches are punishing me. They've stolen those babies." A cackle of laughter spread through the gallery. The faces of the portraits of Van Gogh and Henry James joined the witches.

"You have to help ..." he pleaded but the man had already disappeared.

He ran along the walls of the gallery poking his cane in the eyes of the images hoping to switch off their incessant taunts and laughter.

"We will kill you. We've been waiting for you. We knew you would come," chorused the taunting voices. "Jump off the roof. It is the only way to save yourself. You are part of the underworld, and you must return."

The self-portrait of Van Gogh joined in with the

rhythmical chant. "We will kill you." The Duke of Sherringale stared in horror as blood squirted from Van Gogh's face. Deep vermilion in colour, it seeped from an ear and a gaping mouth, gushing from his eyes.

"Return to the underworld, do it now."

"Jump! Jump! Jump!" The others joined the chant, pointing at him with crooked fingers and bleeding orifices.

"Do it now or you will linger on the fringes of hell for all eternity."

The Duke of Sherringale pulled the cape over his head, his face immobilised with fear.

A door opened and the tentative sound of a woman's voice became apparent through the cacophony of sound.

"Malcolm, hello it's me. Do you remember me, Simone Carter, psychiatrist from the Pines?" She approached him, treading with care until she was alongside him.

"Who's Malcolm? I'm not Malcolm. I am the Duke of Sherringale. You're mistaken." He bolted, stumbling into a corner distracted by the images. His eyes darted from one painting to the next, fear etched into the pores of his skin. He sprang to the far corner of the room and dived over a table with his hands over his head, quaking like a war-ravaged soldier. The door creaked and two policemen entered. Assessing the situation, with legs braced and hands closed round their batons, they stood motionless.

The cavernous mouths of the witches screamed.

"Run to the stairs, climb onto the roof and jump. They'll put you in a cell and throw away the key. Go now. RUN!!"

He turned on the spot with cape flying and ran towards the fire escape. The steel bar gave way as he pushed it down and he clattered up the metal staircase, his breathing laboured. A crimson feather detached from his hat, gently drifting on the breeze.

"They're coming to get you. Run! Run and find the roof."

Although distracted by the voices, the pounding of boots behind him became discernible and he stumbled to the top of the stairs, sprinting through the door into the fresh city air. Reaching the roof he tottered to the edge, slipping on loose roof tiles, using his outstretched arms to balance. For a second, the cool evening air caressed his face, as he heard the beats and rhythms of the brass band below. Music and party blowers infiltrated the sounds of the voices, becoming more urgent, louder, insistent.

"There's no time left. They're following you. They will get you. JUMP!"

Dr Carter approached him, talking in a language he couldn't understand. She seemed to repeat the name Malcolm over and over again.

"Stop it! Stop it now! In the name of God, I'm not Malcolm. I'm the Duke of Sherringale."

"You tell her!" came the voices. "She's an imposter. She doesn't even know your name. Only a few more paces to go and you'll be free. You know what you have to do. It's time for you to fly. GO NOW!"

The Duke of Sherringale inhaled deeply, turned his head towards the psychiatrist and took off. His hand grasped the cane as he jumped into the air. Momentarily, the wind billowed beneath the cape, and he looked as though he might fly. His face relaxed and an exultant smile spread over his face. The group ran to the edge peering over the roof of the building with apprehension.

His head hit the side of a float, cracking open and spilling the contents of his cranium like a broken pinata. Garlands and flowers scattered over his face, music stopped, and the crowd dispersed, horror stamped on their faces. A MIND charity float came to a standstill within inches of his bleeding body.

A myriad of shrill voices reverberated from the gallery. “At last, the Duke of Sherringale has joined the Midsummer Parade.”

The Best Days of Your Life

At the age of seven, Bridget moved with her family to a village in Nottinghamshire. She left a neighbouring primary school and started at another after the Christmas break in 1968.

She had been given the onerous task of accompanying her five-year-old brother Richard to school one snowy January morning. The pair clutched their satchels and dinner money, sliding along the icy pavement to the school, a walking distance of fifteen minutes.

His head hung down like a dying sunflower. He dragged his feet wailing, "I don't want to go to school. I **hate** it."

"Well, you went last week and by Friday you really enjoyed it, mum told me."

"That was last week. I don't like it now. I want my mummy," he whimpered, throwing his brand-new satchel into a puddle. His exercise book tumbled out absorbing the brown muddy water.

"Mummy's at work so you'll have to put up with me for now," Bridget countered, holding the dripping book at arm's length. "What about all the friends you'll make and the games at playtime?"

"Don't like them!" His bottom lip began to tremble, as he scuffed his Start-Rites on the curb, refusing to move. "I'm cold and hun-ger-y."

With some force, Bridget buttoned his coat up to his neck and pulled his cap over his ears. "Why didn't you eat breakfast?"

"There was no toy in the Ricicles box. I wanted to find Dougal. I've got Florence, Brian and Zebedee. Mum said I couldn't open a new box until I'd finished the original packet."

Bridget mopped his tears with the back of her hand and urged him to keep walking. She hunted round in her pocket and found a battered roll of banana Toffos.

"Let's see how long you can chew this without speaking."

"Mummy says we can't have sweets in the morning."

"Well mummy won't know. See who can make it last the longest."

He chewed the toffee with relish, his mouth open displaying the masticated sweet. Relief flowed over her like warm bath water.

Checking her wristwatch, she grabbed his hand, hoping to quicken the pace. The fifteen-minute walk had extended to thirty and they were already fifteen minutes late. She urged him through the school gates as he spat out the Toffo and pleaded, "I want to go home ... per-lease take me home."

Bridget dragged him past her classroom, noticing that all her classmates were seated with Miss Perks pointing at the blackboard with a sharp stick. "Two twos are four, four twos are eight, five twos are ...." The monotone chant rang out as she cajoled Richard to keep walking. Passing the school kitchen, the malodourous odour of stewed meat and custard permeated the air causing her stomach to flip. She was convinced that the slimy liver casserole she had been forced to eat the previous week had caused her stomach upset. She planned to sit next to Graham Bleasby at lunchtime as he had polished off her lunch last week when the dinner ladies' backs were turned. She would swap her food for half an hour with his pet ferret after school.

With Bridget pushing Richard through the porch they made it into his classroom. Wide-eyed five-year-olds stared at them, hands in the air, fingers up their noses demanding the toilet. Bridget pulled at her brother's gloves to remove them and a thwack against his hand caused him to screech in pain. She'd forgotten that the gloves were attached to a long length of elastic which travelled through both sleeves and along his back. His wailing escalated as her attempts to remove him from his outdoor clothing were thwarted and his arms bent into positions that seemed anatomically impossible.

"You're **very** late. What happened?" demanded statuesque Miss French, her arms folded over her ample bosom like a nightclub bouncer.

"He didn't want to come to school today."

"So, where's your mother?" An interrogative tone bled into her words.

"She's at work Miss French. He's been crying."

"Well then, you have to set off earlier tomorrow. You've caused untold disruption, you've both missed registration and the order for this week's school dinners."

Tears stung Bridget's eyes. She couldn't remember who to see about school dinners because her mother had arranged them the previous week.

Richard's cries intensified. He was gasping for breath, pleading with her to take him home. Miss French reminded him that big boys don't cry, took his hand and they both disappeared into a pool of pigtails and plimsolls.

Bridget was relieved; her snivelling brother had been dispatched to the care of Miss French at last. Pelting through the playground she arrived at her classroom breathless and red-faced. With trepidation she knocked on the door.

"Come in!" shouted Miss Perks. She wore a knee-length kilt and a tangerine button- through cardigan. Her hair was the colour of tarmac. Peering over the top of her spectacles, her penetrating stare gnawed at Bridget like a rat through a cable.

"You're late and what have you got stuck to your tie?"

"It's a Toffo Miss."

Bridget's voice was the squeak of a cornered rodent. "I had to take my brother to his class. He didn't want to go."

"You've wasted enough time. Take a seat next to Alan. Are you a green, a red or a yellow?"

"I don't know," her voice faltered, "what does it mean?"

"You should have been put into a group when you joined the class; it must be because you were absent last week. You can be a green for now."

"But what does it ..."

"Enough now!" Miss Perks' pink face glowered.

Bridget scanned the classroom. Her restless classmates were pinching each other, the girls squirting ink from the Quink bottle over crisp white shirts.

"Now where were we, class?" questioned Miss Perks, tapping the blackboard with a stick.

Bridget slipped into the chair next to Alan, put her books on the desk and shrieked as his twelve-inch ruler made contact with her hand.

"I don't like girls, sit somewhere else."

Miss Perks bellowed above the rising cacophony of noise.

"Who was that? Was it you again Bridget? Take your chair and sit facing the wall."

Bridget dodged the pieces of rubber flicked at her as she dragged her chair to the corner of the room.

"**Stop it**!" she shouted, hissing at Tom who had loaded a

catapult with pink and yellow chalk.

"**That's it!** I won't tolerate any more disruption from you Bridget. I don't know what sort of second-rate institution you went to before, but we care about and respect each other here at this school. Take your chair and sit outside. We'll see what the headmaster has to say about this at break time."

All the Time in The World

There are those who know what it's like
to watch their hair disappear down a plughole.

To gaze into a mirror with horror
at the face that stares back.

To witness bloated, blistered skin through
dry eyes, lacking eyelashes or brows.
There are those who know what it's like to be told
refuse this treatment,
and you have less than two years.

There are those who seethe
at well-meaning platitudes.
Live life to the full, stay positive,
Fight your cancer battle bravely.
As though we have a choice.

There are those who scream inside
as family members ask what we do all day.
Who believe we haven't changed at all,
and will be honeymoon fresh

in five years from now.

There are those who can reel off the cheapest plots
and headstones in the locality
who are on first name terms with undertakers
anticipating a card at Christmas.

There are those who throw an ill-fitting wig at the wall,
not wanting to look like Tina Turner.
There are those who know the emergence
of love and support from the unlikeliest of places.

A bunch of daffs left on the doorstep.
Sorry you're having such a bad time
A virtual hug from an old school friend
desperate to visit, an impromptu Zoom call.

The whispered words of a spouse mouthing *I love you*
as a doctor rams a two-inch needle into
your bone marrow.

There are those who *really* see
the joy of a crocus battling to emerge

through a coating of snow.
The one-legged blue tit hanging from a fat ball
whilst filling its beak with mealworm.

There are those who know that, in spite of it all,
the only difference between you and them is
that you know your life is limited, and
they think they have all the time in the world.

Uneasy Lies the Head That Wears the Crown

"You dirty old b…" he bellowed as the amber liquid rained on his head.

"Do you know who I am? Do you …?"

There was no response.

"Well I'll tell you. I am King Alfred of Hawthorne House. A gracious bow is more befitting of someone of my stature, not a thorough drenching."

"He can't hear you, you muppet. Only we can, more's the pity; you do ramble on a bit. Are you going to stand there all day with urine dripping off your crown?" Woody asked.

"That's my business you insignificant little pawn. I take offence at muppet; Your Majesty is more fitting thank you very much. Anyway, how did you manage to avoid the daily downpour Woodentop?"

"Wh- hey you really are from the dark ages. Weren't the Woodentops featured on *Watch with Mother* in the fifties? More like watch with great grandmother in your case; you must be at least eighty. I'd forgotten, weren't you the replacement from the charity shop when they lost the original King? Oh, and by the way, **I** take offence at being called a Woodentop. Granted, I'm made of wood, but I'm a sentient piece of wood with genuine feelings and I'm nobody's puppet."

As they glared at each other a door swung open and a nurse scuttled into the dayroom like a startled cockroach. "No, no no!" Mr Oddpenny, you must **not** urinate in the games corner. How many times do I have to tell you?"

“Oddpenny by name, Oddpenny by nature,” sniggered Woody.

“Let’s zip you up and find a change of clothes, shall we?” With resistance, Mr Oddpenny was escorted towards the bathroom. The rust-coloured stain down the front of his trousers belied a long-term incontinence problem. His slippers squelched as he walked, and he picked at the remains of congealed egg stuck hard to his frayed shirt.

“Nurse Beadle, will you take the chess game and give it a good wash. Put some disinfectant on the carpet too while you’re at it.”

“Yes Staff.”

“Here comes another soaking,” bemoaned King Alfred.

After ten painful minutes, King Alfred and his Queen stood resplendent on their squares. His wooden crown shone like a conker and Bish, Castle and the pawns gazed fixedly into the room.

“Oy pawn. Can you remember when this place was first opened? Must have been 2004 or thereabouts. They got some reality star to cut the ribbon. Those were the days ...”

“My name is not pawn, it’s Woody as it goes,” sneered the pawn.

“This place housed a better class of resident. For a start they didn’t spend all day running on the spot like Jack Threadneedle over there. He wore out a pair of trainers in three months you know and insists on hovering over our board like a Sea King helicopter. Residents were more sedate and dignified back then. They would sit for hours under crocheted blankets squinting through myopic eyes at the crossword with the gentle click and clack of knitting needles in the background.”

"I have noticed that standards have slipped," replied Woody. "Only last week that miserable nurse from Lancet Ward was barking instructions at Tom and Alfie whilst they were napping. Alfie took so long to walk to the toilet she scooped him up in that crusty old wheelie commode and propelled him down the corridor faster than a burglar in a getaway car. Alfie may have only one oar in the water, but he still has some dignity. He was so terrified he started shouting abuse at her and raised his fist; next thing we know he's comatose on the floor with a needle in his arse."

"Alfie's not the only one who drives uphill with the clutch slipping. What about poor old Maisie with her pram full of dolls, rocking them to sleep day and night?"

"My point entirely. I just crave normality. I'm fed up with being an unwitting participant in this circus."

As Woody and Alfred pondered their plight, a cacophony of children's voices intensified as they drew close to the ward. The door was flung open, and twenty pairs of feet skipped into the dayroom. Boys pinched and punched whilst the girls grabbed at each other's pigtails screeching like reconditioned tyres on wet tarmac.

"Children quiet. Don't disturb the oldies."

"Look lively, it's the monthly visit from the infant school," groaned Woody.

"Give me strength. Not another rendition of *There's No-One Quite Like Grandma,* with Hilda crying into her beard," whined Alfred.

"This lot are more likely to mug the old dears than sing to them!"

King Alfred would have nodded if he had the capacity but blinked instead.

The stillness of the afternoon erupted into a whirlwind of shrill laughter and movement. Small arms embraced the more fragrant residents and their teacher's voice splintered the air instructing them to stop fidgeting. The smallest, palest child hopped from side to side, and raised his hand whilst gripping the front of his trousers bleating, "I can't hold on anymore."

"I told you to go before we came out and now you've disrupted everybody Ollie," snapped Miss March. Ollie's bottom lip began to tremble as a teaching assistant dragged him by the hand, annoyed that her pre-concert routine incorporating a dash through a few chromatic scales on the piano had been thwarted.

King Alfred stood motionless, wishing he was somewhere else. Without warning, a small hand lifted him into the air and down into the folds of a dark pocket. His face was squashed into a masticated lump of chocolate and a soiled tissue was scrunched on his head.

"What the ...?" he trilled, "there's something slimy in here." Without success he tried to detach his face from the over-ripe banana peel.

The final notes of Miss Pinchbeck's rendition of "Somewhere Over the Rainbow" accompanied by the piano came to an abrupt end and, with creaking knees, she rose from her stool and lifted her arms to accept the meagre applause.

Miss March trumpeted, "Children! Get into three rows immediately. You're in the second row Tilly and stop fiddling with your cardy." With her right hand poised in the air and her left index finger covering her lips, she hissed "SSSShhhh children."

One downward movement of her hand and the children's faces gurned into rictus smiles. A shaky start to an under-rehearsed version of *The Grand Old Duke of York* in two-part harmony ensued.

Contentious, thought King Alfred, his body bouncing as the child marched up to the top of the hill and marched back down again. Of all the songs to choose, you'd think they'd have given this one a miss given the controversy surrounding the current Duke of York, he mused.

After five painful minutes, the flourish of the final chorus ended in half-hearted applause and King Alfred was yanked out of the pocket by his crown.

"What is this my lad?" hollered a familiar voice. King Alfred, from his lofty position, peered down at the bobbing heads of the children and gasped as Nurse Cruickshank pushed him into Ollie's face.

"I ddd- don't kn-know," quailed Ollie.

"You don't know?" scoffed Nurse Cruickshank.

"This, my boy is a chess piece. The King in fact and you put it into your pocket. Am I right?"

The boy nodded with wide eyes.

"Go and stand in the corner, I don't want to look at your face. You're a common little thief," thundered the nurse.

Ollie dragged his feet as he made his way to the back of the room.

"... and don't dawdle!"

"We don't talk to children like that anymore Nurse Cruickshank, I'll deal with him," intervened Miss March.

"That's the problem with the world today. There's no accountability. Anything goes. Children pocket anything they fancy without being reprimanded. That's why the country's in the state it's in. Your innocent charges become another *snowflake generation* where they burst into tears if their school dinner doesn't have a vegan alternative. It's our duty to create children with a backbone. Believe me it's a tough world out there."

"Miss ... Miss, Ollie's wet himself."

The class turned to see Ollie's shoulders hunched, head bowed and a trail of urine seeping out of his shorts. With short gasps, his body convulsed into a puddle of tears.

"Well done Nurse Cruickshank your intervention really worked. You've single-handedly disrupted the whole programme and upset a vulnerable child. How will the residents cope with the distress of missing out on our Johnny Mathis medley with actions? Just look at the disappointment on their bewildered wrinkled faces."

References:

Henry IV Part Two. William Shakespeare. (1597).

There's No-One Quite Like Grandma. Gordon Lorenz. St Winifred's School Choir (1980).

The Grand Old Duke of York. (1642).

Somewhere Over The Rainbow. Judy Garland. (1938)

DRABBLES

Nine Lives and I Had to Pick This One

"I've told you before. Don't pull the cat's tail Tom."

Tom's angelic five-year-old face grinned at her, and she swept him up into her arms, kissing his neck, drinking in the smell of him.

The cat, cartoon-like, sped away, paws trying to move at speed on the wooden floor.

"I'll put CBBC on and you can watch that for a bit? "

"O-k-a-a-y."

He's too quiet, she pondered realising she hadn't seen him for thirty minutes.

"Where are you?"

"I'm here." He grinned from his blood-stained face, holding the cat's head in one hand and its tail in the other.

The Treatment

“I’ve put you down as a DNA, you’re ten minutes late,” grinned the smiling assassin, Nurse Stitch from Oncology Care.

“I was delayed, the ferry was late and there were no buses to the hospital,” pleaded Emily. “It’s taken two hours to get here.”

“I don’t make the rules. Book another appointment on your way out.”

Centred in the waiting room surrounded by patients, Emily’s visceral screech erupted increasing in force and tempo. Prone on the floor she banged her head against the cold tiles, scratching at her face, again and again.

“Call the on-call psychiatrist - she needs therapy.”

Laughing All The Way

Rising at 5.45am, dizzy with fatigue she fed her cats and slurped tepid tea.

A canopy of mist shrouded the house.

At 5.59am she logged onto the site.

Your queue position is 89,635.

Sighing, she peered through sleep- filled eyes at garlands, stars and ribbons flickering on the screen.

Flashing words appeared – only one hour to wait.

After ninety minutes, her heart accelerated.

Four minutes. Three minutes. Two minutes.

Only one minute to go.

Dancing snowmen pixilate. The screen darkens into a black hole.

She jabs at the keyboard. No response.

Palms sweaty. Loud expletives follow.

And a very merry Christmas to you Tesco - with bells on!

Happy Place

There is a happy place where only children live.

A place where days should be filled with sunshine, sandcastles and ice-cream. No rules, no homework, no rebukes.

A place where you could watch the World Cup Final in peace without fear that if his team loses you won't be back at school until the bruises disappear.

"Where is your happy place?" his beautiful golden teacher asked, as she discovered the cigarette burns on his arms.

"I don't have one," he replied, stifling a cry.

"Well together we will find one."

KATE SHARP

Kate was a Clinical Scientist. She grew up in Lymington and then moved away to spend 35 years working for the NHS in a specialist service, including working as part of the organ retrieval and transplant team for 7 years.

Other more minor activities included a husband, son, daughter, tile import and distribution company and a Kumon maths class. Hobbies encompassed sailing, windsurfing, Civil War Reenactment, sewing, and longbow archery. More lethal skills include cooking and gardening.

As part of Kate's research, she published papers in medical journals, and wrote many reports based on data analytics. but then, on retiring, had no clue how to write for fiction or fun.

To solve this problem, on her retirement and return to Lymington, Kate joined the local Creative Writing class, who have proved to be a great source of inspiration, entertainment and support.

Kate still disappears down an information gathering rabbit hole too often, limiting how many stories actually get written and how much homework is handed in.

Her stories are often mildly murderous, and proof of life for her husband is regularly needed; however, Arthur the dog is doing fine.

Annabel and the Magnetic Charm

Annabel stretched luxuriously in the salon chair and sipped her coffee. She always liked to look her best and tomorrow would be a special day.

The new kitchen had been the final touch to their cottage and all her hard work and planning had finally paid off. The cottage had been one of their dreams for many years and, although isolated from main towns, was near enough to the local villages to mean that they could have a rich social life, at least when Trevor was up to it.

Unfortunately, not everything had been perfect and shortly after they had moved to the cottage, Trevor had suffered heart arrhythmias and had a pacemaker fitted. This had then been followed by a massive heart attack and he was now just about physically recovered from a quadruple heart bypass. Despite all this he had still insisted that he would plan everything; as an ex naval NCO he liked to be in control.

Annabel watched idly as the hairdresser layered colour onto foils to soften and highlight her immaculately cut blond hair.

"How is the house redecoration going?" asked the young hairdresser, expertly gathering hair sections onto the comb.

"It is all finished and perfect thank you. The kitchen fitters got everything just right."

'If she only knew,' she mused, suppressing a smile.

Since Trevor's heart attack, he had become more desperate to control absolutely everything, especially her, dictating who she could have as friends, where she could go, what she could wear. He had even bought her a new sports convertible as a birthday gift but then insisted that she cleaned it after every use, and finally her patience had run out.

Annabel's plan had finally crystallised after one of the cats became unwell.

"We need to take Tigger to the vet, he is really unwell," she had told Trevor, stroking her cat's head as he lay shivering on his cushion, despite the morning sun.

"No need, he will be fine, stop fussing," had been the response from Trevor, as he carried out his regular checks of her phone bills and bank accounts.

It was only late that evening that he had finally conceded that she could take Tigger to the vet.

Three days later Tigger was dead. When she had cried, he had responded.

"Stop making such a fuss. Tigger was only a cat. Go buy yourself a new dress or something so we can go out."

Annabel had kept making allowances for him for what seemed like months, reasoning that his increasingly erratic temper and desire for more and more control over her life was related to his loss of control over his own physical wellbeing.

Finally, after he had blocked her from seeing her best friend and refused to go out to a party at the last minute, she had had enough.

"Yes dear," had been her meek but disinterested response, when Trevor had wanted to plan the new kitchen.

"You choose, but please could we have a kitchen island, and I really would like an induction hob rather than gas, as it would be so much easier to keep clean. Have you seen that really elegant one with the removable magnetic control knob? It fits virtually flush with the worktops and gives a beautifully sleek finish."

The kitchen had taken longer than expected to be fitted and at times she had wondered if she had got the right units and configuration, especially as Trevor liked to do most of the cooking.

The result had been worth the wait. New kitchen units in modern contrast colours were in place, and the island was placed well so that there was space to walk past it all round, although it was a little tight near the hob.

After the workmen had left and they had done the final cleaning and sat down, Annabel had said,

"Let me cook dinner tonight, to celebrate, so that you don't overstrain yourself."

As expected, Trevor had insisted that he should do the cooking; at times she thought he was deliberately trying to fatten her up so that she would be less attractive to other men. That evening, however, he announced he would make a stir fry.

"Have you checked the instructions on how to use the hob?" he asked her, as she dutifully helped out, chopping and slicing ingredients and assembling them in small dishes ready for him.

"Yes, it is really easy" she responded.

"Basically, once it is turned on, the big control knob just needs to be tilted towards the area of the hob you want to use and then twisted clockwise or anticlockwise to change the heat settings. You will feel the pans vibrate slightly as the induction field takes effect. I suggest you use the large front ring on 'max' to get the best heat."

Trevor selected the new wok they had bought to be compatible with the hob from the cupboard, and checked that he had all the ingredients he needed arranged neatly, then added oil and onion to the pan and set it to gently sizzle.

"Would you like a glass of wine?" she asked, moving from the stool on which she was perched towards the fridge near the hob.

Trevor grunted assent as he continued to add ingredients, turning up the heat more as the beef strips went in, to achieve perfect searing.

"Excuse me," she said as she wriggled behind him to reach for the glasses in the top cupboard, causing him to move closer to the hob.

"It's a bit hot in here," he said, as he continued to stir, and accepted the wine gratefully.

"Not really," she said, "But I can open the patio door if that would help."

A memory of Tigger meowing as he had waited so often to come through that door hardened her resolve.

Trevor sat down suddenly on a bar stool, his face pale and grey and his lips blue, a fine sheen of sweat coating his skin.

Annabel was happy to help. It seemed as if things were going well this evening. As she walked over to him with her glass of wine she said,

"If you were to sit on a bar stool next to me, by the hob, you could advise how I should do the rest of this."

"Thanks," he said, moving unsteadily back to sit near her.

As the pan heat increased the stir fry took shape. The control knob was easy to use and the wok vibrated under her hand as she increased the induction setting to maximum.

Beside her Trevor started to say something, then gasped and slid off his stool to the floor.

"Are you OK? Is it your heart?" she said, turning down the

heat and folding her hand around the hob control.

She knelt over him, putting her hand to his chest. Trevor's heart rate grew more and more erratic and then stopped.

Annabel pushed herself off the floor and called 999.

When the ambulance crew arrived she was doing CPR. The hob had switched itself off and the stir fry was cooling in the pan.

She looked exhausted. Response times were, as she knew from his previous heart attack, slow this far out.

The paramedics examined Trevor and shook their heads sadly.

"Sorry Madam, there is nothing we can do. Is there anyone we can call for you?"

The post-mortem had concluded that Trevor's pacemaker had failed, and he had had a catastrophic heart attack.

Annabel was pleased that her hair would look really good for the funeral; she was looking forward to an independent future.

Back in the kitchen, the shiny new induction hob gleamed quietly under the extractor hood lights, the power off and the removable magnetic knob sitting innocently back in place.

RTFM, thought Annabel.

Marriageable?

Astur was 9 years old. Her parents had moved to the UK from Somalia in the 1980s to escape the civil war. Now, in 1997, the country was more peaceful, and her mum said she wanted to go back and visit her relatives in Mogadishu over the school summer break and would take Astur with her for a holiday.

Prior to the trip she excitedly looked up information on the country.

"I'm going to Africa for the summer," Astur told her best friends, Emma and Jodi.

"Mum says we can go to the beach and the Union Mosque and maybe even the Rashke Barre wildlife park."

"Has it got lions and tigers?" said Emma.

"No silly," Jodi interrupted. "Tigers come from India."

"Well, it will have hippos and lions and giraffes and elands I think," said Astur.

"What's a Mosque like?" said Jodi. "We haven't got any near us in Ashbourne."

"I'll send you some pictures and we can chat every evening."

Astur's teacher, Mrs Aspen, was very pleased.

"You can come back next term and tell us all about it."

Packing done, vaccinations over with, Astur's dad drove them to Heathrow. Once they arrived in Mogadishu they were going to stay with her aunts on the outskirts of the city.

“You had better leave your camera at home,” said Idil.

“But Mum, I promised to get my friends pictures,” Astur complained.

Idil dropped her eyes.

“You won’t have anywhere to get photos developed where we are staying, and anyway the cost would be too high. You can talk to your friends when you get back.”

Astur was glad they were finally going. Her mum and dad had been arguing a lot in the last few months and Astur had been unsure what was upsetting them. It sounded as if it was a debate about ‘customs and marriageability’, whatever that was, and what other people would think.

“When you come home you will be a woman,” her dad assured her as she got out of the car.

Now Astur was back at home.

The pain was constant, she couldn’t sit down comfortably, and she couldn’t wee properly anymore. Her aunts had told her that she was going to see a wise woman for a special ceremony. They had gagged her and held her down, telling her that it was for her own good and no man would trust her or marry her if it wasn’t done.

It was perfectly legal.

She had bled a lot and then there had been infection. There had not been any wildlife park or time on the beach. Astur and her mum had stayed in Africa for the whole summer holiday until she had partially healed, and the stitches were out.

These days she didn’t chat with the other girls at break,

and she couldn't tell her teacher.

Now she needed a doctor, and her family would not take her.

Her future of pain was assured.

"But at least you will get a husband," they told her.

Astur didn't understand.

I Can Spell Really Well

I can spell really well. It's not something you really expect these days.

I discovered my ability by accident when I was 9 years old. School had shown us a film about an American girl who had changed her life by winning spelling competitions, first at school and then nationally. Our school decided to hold a Spelling Bee and my form teacher suggested that I should join in.

As you may have guessed, I am a social misfit in school, firstly because I am fat and secondly because I wear glasses and am a nerd. I thought perhaps that if I did well in the competition, I would at least get less teasing and bullying.

In lunchbreak I went into the library and found a book I thought might help called 'The modern spell dictionary'. I checked it out and stuffed it in my bag for later.

On my way home Chelsea and her make-up covered friends were bunched together near the gate and, as usual, had a go at me.

"Oh look. It's that stupid fat bitch."

"Teacher's pet."

"Four-eyed nerd."

I hunched my shoulders and plodded past them. There was no point in replying.

Mum had made macaroni cheese for tea, so I was feeling quite cheerful when I went up to my room to start on homework.

First though, I thought I would have a proper look at the book I had taken out. In the film the girl had got much better at spelling when she knew the meanings of the words.

I opened the book at random.

The first word I spotted was 'Soften': make or become soft or softer, make or become less severe.

I flipped the pages again.

'Enhance': intensify, increase or further improve the quality, value or extent of.

'Interrupt': stop the continuous progress of (an activity or process).

Each definition was accompanied by an odd square of dots which I thought looked like a QR code.

I had heard of QR codes but never really been sure of what they did or how to use them, so I wondered what they were doing in the dictionary.

I turned back to the beginning of the dictionary.

'Instructions'.

'For best results use the QR code below on your smartphone to go to and download the free spell dictionary app.'

I followed the instructions and once the app was uploaded a message came up.

'To use the app, look up a word, check its meaning and then point the camera and click on the QR code. Press the code again to halt the process.'

Very odd.

I looked out of the window at a blackbird in the garden.

This time I clicked on the QR code next to 'Quieten': make or become silent, calm, or still.

Suddenly the blackbird, which had been beaking for

worms on the lawn while making its usual noisy racket, became quiet and still.

Coincidence, I thought, and tried it on next door's Jack Russell terrier.

For what felt to me like the first time ever, the horrid little thing stopped yapping and lay down.

This can't be real, I thought, and went downstairs to watch 'The Simpsons' with my sister.

The next day, however, was really good fun.

Firstly, I looked up 'Soften' again and reduced Chelsea and her friends to a heap of slug-like blobs on the ground.

I tried 'Crabs' on the RE teacher who liked to grope boys and girls.

'Alopecia' worked well on the boy who was convinced he could charm any girl because he looked good and who had then dumped my big sister.

This was great entertainment and I decided to do a celebratory selfie with my friend Joanne.

I then pointed the phone at my loose change and pressed 'Multiply'.

"Oops"

Now there are at least 25 of me.

Double Jeopardy

"Can I add vodka to the Tesco's order?".

"For heaven's sake! What do you want that for? We are drowning in alcohol, and we don't need any more rubbish in this house."

Ben turned back to his sudoku, disregarding her as usual.

"I thought it would be a good idea for cleaning jewellery and other bits around the house. I've been reading about older remedies for household problems."

As Annie predicted, Ben snapped back at her.

"More stupid eco rubbish. At least get gin, then I can always drink it and it won't get wasted."

Annie grinned surreptitiously – gin would do at a pinch, although vodka would have done a better job.

She made a mental note to look up composting next.

"What else do we need for this week's order?

"Well, we have enough of all the tins, you don't need any more pasta, we've got too much cheese and what do you need cream for?"

The conversation dissolved into the usual dispute about what could be bought.

Eventually, with the order signed off, Annie swung the conversation to the plan for the next few days.

"Are you doing archery this week?"

"Yes, Thursday afternoon. Why don't you take the dog out and get him to practice walking properly on the Halti for once?"

Annie agreed. Although she hated being told what to do,

this would fit in beautifully with her plans.

"Perhaps I'll take him to the churchyard, visit mum's grave and then take him through to the field at the back."

Wednesday came. Tesco delivered, and for once there were no substitutions. Not even aubergines as a swap for asparagus.

While Ben was working Annie went into the garden. She needed a large glass container.

Ben had just dumped two perfectly good demijohns into the glass collection box and had made her throw away all the spare glass jars she had saved for use later. However, the week before Annie had found a half gallon glass bottle which had been sitting behind the greenhouse. The inside was scruffy and had some green slime and old leaves in the bottom and it was half full of rainwater, but it would be perfect for what she needed.

Thursday afternoon, Ben took his electric car, and she took her scruffy old Citroen – the 'you don't really need that car' that she had been allowed to keep. She drove down to the car park and, telling Fredo to jump down, she walked through to the churchyard. In addition to pooh bags she carried a plastic bag, heavy scissors, and a folding carrier bag.

The churchyard was quiet and, with a thought that her mum would approve of what she was doing, Annie stripped yew leaves and berries from the old tree by the church, sliding her gloved hands against the twigs to strip off the leaves, while Fredo sniffed around interestedly, sampling the smells on the tree trunk.

Once home again, Annie tipped the old water and leaves out of the glass bottle in the garden, poured in the yew leaves and berries, and covered them with the bottle of gin, sealing the top of the bottle with cling film and hiding it back behind the green house.

Going back indoors, Annie carefully broke the gin bottle and put the bits into the glass recycling. If Ben asked, she could always say she had dropped it.

The rest of the afternoon Annie spent hoovering, running the dishwasher, washing machine and tumble dryer, so that she could keep up with the housework without a lecture on why she was making a noise or using the machines too much.

While she had a cup of coffee, Annie flicked through screens of information on her phone, going back to the article she had been reading on optimal extraction of ricin from kidney beans. She had known that undercooked beans would be toxic but had found a brilliant article in which it said slow cooking at 80 C would increase toxicity five-fold. She put dried beans in to soak.

The next day the chilli she made in the slow cooker smelled really good. She split it into two batches, knowing that Ben would then complain that again she had made too much in one go and that there wasn't enough space in the freezer.

She carefully labelled one dish as slow cooker chilli and put it in the freezer, choosing the wrong drawer just to annoy him.

The rest of the chilli she transferred to a saucepan and boiled thoroughly before serving and enjoying it for dinner.

The following week followed its usual pattern. Arguments over the dishwasher, washing machine, Tesco order, Ben opening her mail and reading her phone messages.

Tuesday came and Ben announced he was 'going off to a business meeting' and would stay overnight with friends.

As soon as he left, Annie put on the washing machine and laundered all Ben's socks and pants. While they were drying, she brought in the soaked yew leaves and berries from the garden, strained off the gin through a coffee filter and found a large glass bowl. She added in Ben's pants and socks and then spread them out on plastic tray to let the gin evaporate off.

The underwear soon dried out and she sprayed them with Febreze to remove any lingering scent of gin, then put them back in his drawer.

A week later Ben was feeling a bit off colour. He complained that he had cramps in his legs and stomach the night before and that his vision was a bit odd, and he had odd heart beats. Annie reassured him that perhaps he needed a little more salt in his diet and suggested he cleaned his contact lenses. She told him that his sleepiness must be because he was working so hard.

Annie thought, 'it's time to move things along a little.'

She thawed the slow cooked chilli.

That evening Annie said that she was a bit nauseous and had an upset tummy.

"I am just hoping I don't have Norovirus. They had signs up in the outpatient clinic yesterday. I think I'll just have some cereal tonight. Is your chilli ok?"

"Fine thanks. I suppose I will be eating it for the next few days since you don't like it."

Annie said to herself, 'not if I have anything to do with it.'

After dinner Ben muttered, "I am really feeling a bit rough this evening."

He rubbed his belly. "Perhaps I ate too much rice?"

Annie snorted quietly to herself 'Perhaps he ate too much ricin.'

"Just sit back and let me clear up."

An hour later Ben was unconscious.

Annie called an ambulance 4 hours later.

"He said he had stomach-ache," she told the first responders. "And I wondered if he had Norovirus?" she continued. "He went to sleep on the settee as usual, but then I couldn't wake him up."

At the hospital they took off Ben's clothes, leaving his underpants on him, giving the rest back to Annie while they put him in a hospital gown. They suggested she should go home while they did some tests.

The doctors phoned and asked if there was anything unusual that he had eaten.

"We just had chilli as we often do."

Annie carried on celebrating, by putting on the washing machine and tumble dryer. In no time at all Ben's underwear was completely clean and dry.

The doctors could not understand Ben's worsening symptoms. Some suggested that he might have ricin toxicity and he was treated on that basis. They expected that he should recover, but he seemed to have severe unexplained cardiovascular and ocular symptoms and lapsed into heart block. He died a couple of days later.

At the post-mortem the toxicity screen done in the local lab showed up the presence of ricin and this was listed as the cause of his accidental death.

As Annie had predicted, the yew taxines he had absorbed through the skin from his socks and pants would have only shown up if the samples had been sent to a specialist lab, but as ricin had been found locally no further screens were carried out.

As Annie completed her Tesco order, she thought:

‘It’s really silly, the things that will drive you to murder.’

Tension

Sandra was late for work.

She had resorted to desperate measures to get out of the door in time to get to the bus stop.

Storm Elspeth pummelled the streets.

Sandra's feet were soaking, wet skirt clinging to her legs under her jacket, and her hair in 'rats-tails', by the time she reached the pneumatic doors of the double decker.

"Good morning, Miss, usual stop?" grinned the driver.

"Yes please."

Sandra pulled out her soggy bus pass, while hitching at her clothes with the other hand. She squelched across to the nearest seat and pondered on how the day had gone so wrong this early. OK, she should have set her alarm properly. Making her packed lunch last night would have helped, and she really should have put the laundry on two days ago, so that it would have had a chance to dry.

The bus lurched and Sandra's bag fell off the seat, spilling papers everywhere. As she bent over to retrieve her stuff, she felt things slipping and grabbed at her waist again.

"Here you are love," said an elderly lady in the seat across the aisle and handed her back a now grubby bundle of notes.

"Thanks," said Sandra, wriggling slightly as she reached across to grasp the proffered sheets.

"This is my stop," she said, stuffing the papers into her bag and struggling to her feet, while clutching everything frantically.

Once off the bus, progress towards work was erratic and

unusual.

In one hand Sandra held her bulging bag, and with the other she continued to clench at her midriff, giving her a strange, hunched shuffle as she headed towards the front door of her office building.

OK, she was indoors now, but Geoff, her office mate, was already at his desk with a clear view of the clothes pegs and her desk. How could she take her coat off without letting go? She wriggled and struggled and finally removed the coat and tried to hang it up.

"Whatever are you doing?" asked an astonished Geoff, who had watched her contortions.

Through the glass wall of the office, she saw her boss approaching the door and simultaneously felt the slither as lacy fabric pooled round her ankles.

Geoff sniggered.

Sandra flushed a delicate shade of pink.

Her boss gaped.

She would not have been in this pickle if she had not had to try to dry her damp underwear in the microwave. Sandra had seen this method used for warming towels in the Indian Restaurant. Obviously, she had not tried to dry her bra as it had metal underwires. That would be as silly as microwave drying your poodle.

Unfortunately, the power setting of 1000 watts for 3 minutes was not beneficial to knicker function.

When microwaved, elastic smoulders and then goes crunchy.

Conflict in the Gym

There was a ghost in the running machine, Freda was sure of it.

The svelte, super-toned gym instructor examined her perfectly manicured fingernails and said in a tone of bored indifference,

"To programme the running machine, start by pressing clear on the keypad and then choose programme one."

What she didn't say, but Freda could hear the unspoken thought, was:

"You know, the programme for fat blobs like you, who wouldn't be so fat if they stopped stuffing their greedy faces for five minutes."

Freda wanted a bun!

She had promised herself that if she signed up to gym, she would get thinner.

The spiteful running machine was determined to make it difficult for her, as it never did as it was told.

Freda had always been too fat. Currently she was using her old Weight Watchers books, assigning points to everything she ate, being totally miserable and forcing herself to go to the gym. This morning it had been raining hard and blowing a gale, so by the time she got to the gym Freda was soaking wet, her hair hanging in stringy tails and dripping down the back of her neck. Changing at the gym was out of the question – other people would see how fat and ugly she was and would sneer – so her gym clothes were wet through before she even started.

Freda drew a big breath, peered at the screen on the running machine again, and pressed what she thought was the right button.

Unfortunately, she had taken off her glasses before she started, as they always steamed up when she got hot, so she wasn't quite sure which button was which.

The machine beeped at her, but the rubber mat thing wouldn't budge.

"Look, let me set it up for you," said the instructor.

"You press this one here – 'Clear', then that one. It's simple. I'll stand behind you until you get sorted out."

Freda was tired and wet and cold and angry. She poked vindictively at the buttons and then pressed Start. The programme began and the rubber mat started to move. Outside she could hear thunder through the rattle of the rain on the windows.

Rapidly the machine picked up pace, making her start to walk faster and faster and then run.

"I think you may have pressed the advanced programme," said the gym bitch from behind her, who then muttered under her breath, "You stupid fat cow."

Freda, by this time, was a large sweating, heaving mass.

Fate intervened. An extra loud clap of thunder startled her, making her desperately clutching hands lose their grip on the machine.

'F=MA', thought Freda, as she flew backwards off the speeding machine at high speed.

The flat gym instructor said nothing.

ESTER SPILLER

Ester Spiller was born in rural Kwa-Zulu Natal, South Africa. She has always liked writing because the characters in stories tend to be a lot easier to understand than the characters in real life. In 2016 she moved to the United Kingdom with her husband, children and pets.

Ester published her first novel, Sexing the Crocodile, in 2021. Other short pieces have been published in several anthologies and some of her work is included in publications at God's House Tower in Southampton. In 2023 she came 8th out of more than 5000 writers in the NYC Midnight 250-word micro fiction competition. Ester is currently teaching a creative writing course through Brockenhurst College while doing her MA in Creative Practice.

A man's work is never done

"That's enough now Small, stop your fussing."

"But Grumpa why can the girls—" Small's wailing turned the rest of the sentence into a garbled mess, but Grumpa understood the despair unfairness caused in young minds. Grumpa also knew the world refused to change, even for the tears shed by tiny humans.

"That's enough now." Grumpa patted the curly blond head.

Small buried his face in the green tartan blanket that covered his grandfather's lap, and kept sobbing. A few short months ago he would have tried to crawl up onto Grumpa's lap, but now he was older he just tried to melt into the space next to the wheelchair, hoping the girls wouldn't see him in this state.

"Alright, alright, come now, come now my pet. That's enough now," Grumpa said gently, stroking his rough hands over Small's hair. "Come, help me with the vegetables and I'll tell you a story about The Great War."

Small sniffled for a few more minutes and then looked up. Grumpa told really good stories.

"Go on, fetch me the bowl and vegetables."

Small walked back carefully with the vegetables and made another trip for the water and the knives. He sat down next to Grumpa, the mound of vegetables next to him. Although he was only five his hands were already nimble with a paring knife. He knew while he peeled and scraped Grumpa would keep talking.

"Now, when the war started, you had to go to the doctor to see what job you were fit to do in the army. He would—"

Small giggled.

“And what’s the giggle for little man?” Grumpa knew what the giggle was for.

“You said *he*. Boys can’t be doctors Grumpa.”

“Oh yes they can.”

Small just shook his head, making his curls bounce.

“Well, you may be right, they can’t *now*, but boys could be doctors *before* the war. When I was a lad your age, boys could be whatever they wanted to be. Anything. The boss in a factory, the owner of a store, even lawyering or doctoring, anything. Fancy jobs, lowly jobs. Any jobs.”

Small giggled some more. He loved Grumpa’s crazy stories.

“When the war came all the able-bodied boys were shipped off to go and kill other boys they had never met. The women, they stayed home, weathering out the bombs, bringing up the children. Guns and ammunition had to be made to feed the hungry war machine. Farms had to be run to feed everyone. Someone had to do all the jobs the men left behind. So, the women stepped up. Into jobs they had never done before. They learned fast. Soon they were running the workforce.”

Grumpa nodded sagely. Small was still trying to picture a male doctor.

“Then the war ended. And the boys came back. Not all of them mind. So many rotted under the poppies in foreign soil. Some lost a limb. All of them lost a part of their mind. Them boys that came back were different than the ones that left. Look at a photo and you’d say *oh yes, that’s him, Jimmy, my friend, we grew up together.* But the Jimmy with light in his eyes, Jimmy always up for a laugh, that was not the Jimmy that came back to his mum’s house. New Jimmy walks with a shrapnel limp, jumps at loud noises and drinks every day. That’s not the boy I played conkers with, you think. That's an old broken man wearing a young man's face.

"The boys came home, and they wanted to go back to their old jobs, but they found there was already someone in the seat. They went to the bosses to complain. But the bosses just smiled their lipstick smiles and said, 'Sorry, the position's been filled, we will let you know if anything suitable comes up.'

"The boys got very angry. There was a huge uproar. Then that lady, what was her name? Ah yes, Elenor Fick. She started making them films, all about men and how they weren't really suited for certain jobs. Women were just *genetically predisposed* to be better at engineering and all that hog. And how their hormones made men snap too easily, and that's what started the war in the first place. There was all this talk about how the war had made men weak, and now they can't be near loud noises and certain smells because it might break their frail constitutions. And that was the nail in the coffin. The movies. People started believing what the Fick flicks were saying. Never mind that they had lived through another truth. Memories are funny things, aren't they?"

Small sat cross legged on the floor, peeling another potato. This story wasn't for him anymore.

"I'll never forget, one day, in the thick of it, having a right go at my mam. She was running the big steelworks by then, over Scunthorpe way.

'Why are you doing this Mum?!' I was making a right fool of myself, shouting at her like that, 'Your own son can't even get a job. They tell me all I'm suited for is cleaning the house. Cleaning the house? In this thing?'

'What if you get married boy? Your wife won't want you out of the house for such long hours, too tired to cook a decent dinner when she gets home.'

'What wife would want a man in a wheelchair anyway? It's all upside-down Mum...'

She turned to me with that, ice cube down the spine, stare. That woman could shut you right up without words. She didn't raise her voice, she just lit up a fag.

'*We* didn't choose this, son, *you* did. No woman wanted that war. You grew up in this house, remember how it was? Me, always a bun in the oven, trying to feed you lot with a turnip and an onion while the pay check went down his throat. Always better with his fists than his words, your dad. *For King and country,* he said. But I knew he was thinking of those *foreign* girls. How many little bastard brothers do you think you have running around?

'No, no woman ever wanted war. Sons and brothers gone. For what? Where is the glory in starving children at home? Their Da, a photo on the mantel. When a typing job came up at the steelworks, I jumped at it. Anna cut her teeth at my desk. She learned to read upside down looking at me drafting letters.

'No, we are not doing this to you, you did it to yourselves. Your forefathers had it all. They pissed it away. Now it's *our* turn. I wish I could give you a chance my son, I know you're clever enough, but we can't risk it you see. We can't risk it going back the way it was.'

"And that was it, end of discussion. I was lucky to meet your grandma, willing to take a man in a chair. You see Small, life's not fair. If you want to blame anyone, blame your great-granddad for all this nonsense.

"Now go splash some water on your face. The girls will be home from school soon and here's us chatting away like a bunch of old roosters. The beds still need making and there's nothing on the stove yet. Come, come. A man's work is never done!"

*

Small looked at the mottled mirror after he splashed water on his face. Grumpa was always full of stories; you never knew which were real and which were make believe. According to Grumpa there were imps living under his bed who crept out at night and stole his hair for knitting scarves; that was why Grumpa had almost no hair left on his head. There were plenty hairs in his ears and nose though; maybe ear and nose hairs weren't suitable for scarves, Small thought. Grumpa also said if you eat while lying down you would grow horns. Small was more worried about choking. Horns sounded wonderful; he could use them against the bigger girls when they bullied him.

*

When Small asked older people, "What is that?", they would say, "Horses with long ears."

"Aren't horses with long ears just donkeys?" he asked.

"No. Now go do your chores."

Small looked through the picture books, looking for a horse with long ears, but he never found one.

Grumpa never said horses with long ears; he waited until the two of them were alone and explained what was happening, as best he could, to Small. That's how Small knew why the lady dog had to be locked up sometimes; it had nothing to do with horses, or long ears.

Grumpa also never said, "Leave, its women's."

Leave its women's meant many things. It meant, don't touch that, boys are not allowed. It meant, this topic is not open for discussion. It meant, you won't understand. It meant, I don't want to explain. But mostly it meant, shut up and do what you're told.

The men said it with fear. The women said it with authority.

Leave its women's.

Even though Small was very young, he knew there were certain things you kept in your mind until you had a moment alone with Grumpa. Grumpa was good with horses with long ears, and he was great with women's things. That was probably why Grumpa secretly taught Small how to read. Even the threat of jail or death couldn't keep him from seeing the joy on his grandson's face when he decoded the secrets and mysteries held between the covers of books. Small promised on the head of his favourite dolly, on the pudding of a thousand Sundays, on the lives of his unborn children, that he would never, ever, let on that he could read. If anyone found out, he would never, never, never, ever, ever, ever tell them that it was Grumpa who taught him. Not in a million years. Small practised saying that he picked it up from watching his sisters. He practised that so often he believed it. The story was completely plausible. Small was quick on the uptake, too clever for a boy, his mum always said. If they found out that he could read it would be an inconvenience; if they found out Grumpa taught him, it would be trouble, *big* trouble. You can't un-teach a child to read.

*

The day was hot, especially for spring. All the men in the neighbourhood gathered under the big oak tree in the park to do the mending. The smaller children played on the swings and in the sandpit. Most of the older boys played with them, under the guise of babysitting. All the older girls were in school. Small sat in front of Grumpa, unpicking an old jumper. When it was done, he held his hands shoulder width apart, while Grumpa looped the hank of wool around them, then Grumpa wound the wool off his hands into a ball. This gave Small a lot of time to listen to the old men without being accused of being underfoot; useful boys could learn a lot, if they were quiet.

While the men gossiped and laughed, he saw Uncle Farra scribble something in a tiny book that he quickly secreted back into his sleeve, believing no one saw him. Small realised that, if Grumpa's stories were true, all the old men should be able to read and write. Grumpa said he couldn't teach Small to write yet; it was too dangerous, there would be too much proof. If only he could see the little book Uncle Farra hid up his sleeve, he could know for sure.

*

The opportunity came about, quite by chance, the next week, when Grumpa sent Small to the shop with Uncle Farra. It wasn't easy to get around the shop in the wheelchair, so Small was often sent on errands with adults, when they needed some things for the house. Small could be trusted to mind his elders and not be too much trouble. Uncle Farra was known for his sharp tongue and his quick pinch. He didn't really like children, not even his own grandchildren, but he didn't mind Small, probably because one didn't always notice when he was there, and you could easily forget that Small was a child. He was just part of the scenery.

"What does that say Uncle Farra?" Small pointed to a sign outside the shop. He watched the old man's eyes dart over the words.

If it was any other child, Uncle Farra would have given them a clip around the ear for asking such a potentially dangerous question, but to Small he just said, "Leave, its women's."

The sign read: Tomatoes half off.

Uncle Farra bought double the usual number of tomatoes.

So, he can read, Small thought.

"Why are you buying so many tomatoes?" Small asked innocently.

"I want to make chutney." Uncle Farra narrowed his eyes at Small. *There's no flies on this one*, he thought, *too clever for a boy.*

*

Small watched the other old men too. They all did the same when they saw words; their eyes read quickly, their mouths said, "Leave its women's."

One day, when they were alone, Small asked Grumpa, "Can all men read?"

Grumpa let his eyes wander around for a while, making sure there was no one else around. "No. Most my age can. They couldn't do anything about that. There was one night, before your father was born, we woke up from the smell of the fires. They burned so many books that terrible night. The next day, there were no more boys in schools, there were new laws. The male teachers and professors, they were gone. We were told they were needed elsewhere. I've heard stories," Grumpa shrugged, "But you know, you want to keep your family safe, so you don't listen to too many stories. You don't ask too many questions. And now we are here, none of your friends can read, none of them even think about reading." Grumpa cupped Small's face in his rough, gnarled hands. "My darling child. You will be surprised how quickly things can change when you introduce fear. It is like a hungry ferret in a cage full of little mice. People will do anything to survive, even things that will not serve them in the long run."

Small got up and gave his Grumpa a long hug.

Grumpa's story made Small even more determined to figure out when the reading stopped. When he was around men a little older than his father he watched them closely too. When they came across words they would frown and tilt their heads. Like when you see someone at a train station and you can't quite place them. You don't know if they're famous, or someone you went to school with; either way, you're too shy to walk up to them and ask.

When he asked his father about the words, the answer was a dismissive, "Leave its women's."

The boys his age didn't even look at words. What use did they have for such strange markings? When he asked his friend Marko why he never tried to read, Marko frowned and said, "I dunno, its women's," like the very idea of written down words belonged to women.

*

There weren't many books in the house where Small lived with his sisters, mother, father and Grumpa. There weren't many books in any homes for that matter. His sisters brought books home from school and if they wanted to get more books they could go to the Women's Centre. Having home libraries wasn't exactly illegal, but it was highly discouraged. There *were* books for boys, books with detailed pictures of recipes, house chores and how to mend clothes. You still had to learn things, even if you weren't allowed to read.

There was a limited number of picture books that told fairy stories. Small's favourite was the one about Little Red Cap, who was supposed to take bread and wine to his sick grandfather, but then he listened to the wolf and got eaten for his troubles.

When his mother tried to take the books away from Small, Grumpa said, "Leave him, it's only pictures."

Until one day Mother caught him looking at a book that had no pictures.

"Why are you looking at that book, Small?" She cocked her head suspiciously.

Small's heart was pounding, "I dunno. I like the way it looks, I like thinking about what it could say?"

"And what do you think it says?" His mother wasn't born yesterday.

"Nothing. Something about Princes and castles and shoes and dragons maybe?" Small wasn't born yesterday either, he was six now.

*

Uncle Farra was the head charman at the Women's Centre. He ruled his little army of cleaning men like a general; the place gleamed. Even though Small was a bit too young Grumpa pulled some strings and got him a job, helping Uncle Farra. He was nimble, and happy to climb quite high to do the dusting in hard-to-reach corners. Especially in the library.

Small *borrowed* books from the library, although the library didn't exactly know about it. Small figured it was okay because he brought them back in the same condition he got them, and in the prescribed time. He didn't technically have a card but then again, he couldn't technically read, so it all squared off. Small loved the books, he found himself in the books, parts of him he didn't even know existed. He went with the brave girls on quests in far off lands, into caves with treasure and perilous sea voyages. He was there with them, on their wild adventures, while being stuck in a place where he was only good for dusting and peeling and caring for sticky screaming children. Small lived more in those books than he did in his own body.

It was all gravy baby, as Grumpa would say.

Until the day of the chameleon.

The day the librarian's friend came in with the beautiful curly tailed beast perched on a twig, in a bird cage. They had found it in a container full of fruit from halfway across the world. She needed a book on how to keep the chameleon alive.

"Oh look! A cha-me-lee-on!" Small said, his eyes sparkling with wonder.

"A what?" the librarian asked.

"A cha-me-lee-on. That one looks like the panther cha-me-lee-on from Madagascar."

"Why are you saying it like that?"

"Like what?"

"Cha-me-lee-on, that's not how it's pronounced, it's a chameleon. Where did you learn to say it like that?"

"I read about them in—" Small smacked his hands over his mouth like he could force the words back into his mouth. His eyes went big and scared.

The two dangerous women looked at Small with amused head tilts.

"You read it, you say?" the librarian prodded again.

"No, no, no, no, no. I heard it, I meant to say. I heard it. On the T.V. The other day. The woman with the animals. Dianne Attenburough, she went, to the place. To Madagascar. She saw those things." Small pointed at the chameleon. "She said it, and I heard it, on the T.V."

The librarian's friend raised her eyebrow. "If you heard it on the T.V. you would know it was pronounced chameleon and not cha-me-lee-on."

"I had an ear infection last year?" Small asked hopefully.

The librarian looked at Small, and then at her friend. She looked at them in a way that you could see a lot of cogs were turning; she was making many decisions in a short space of time. Small was eyeing them like a mouse eyeing something that could be a ferret. The ball of adrenaline in his stomach balancing between fight, flight or freeze.

The women communicated without talking out loud. Then the librarian looked at the door. It was still early and there were only three other women in the library, a mother reading to her small daughter and a student, writing fast, a whole stack of books next to her. No one had heard the exchange with Small.

The librarian pursed her lips and said, "Come with me." She motioned to Small and her friend to follow her to the office. If there was a time to run, it was now, but Small simply couldn't run. Even in his few short years of life, the idea that you could say no to woman was already scared out of him. He followed the women to the office.

The librarian locked the door behind them.

Small's heart was beating in his ears. He was so scared he felt faint. He should have made a run for it. He should have run and run and run. As far away as his legs could carry him. He should have joined the circus, joined a band, joined anyone that would have him. Anywhere but here. He had no idea what his punishment was going to be but he was on the verge of wetting himself.

As if she read his mind the librarian turned and said, "Don't be afraid."

That didn't help at all. Small started crying silently.

"Stop it." The librarian shook Small lightly. "Stop it, I'm not going to hurt you."

"You're, hurting, me, right, now," Small sobbed.

The librarian stopped shaking Small and gave him a quick hug. "I'm so sorry, I didn't mean to scare you. I just didn't want us to get caught."

"But you're not smoking?" Small thought of the cigarettes Grumpa snuck behind the house when he thought no one was looking.

The librarian laughed. "No, I would never smoke in a library. I was scared of getting caught talking to you about reading."

Small's eyes went big again.

"It's fine, it's okay, we're not going to tell anyone," the librarian's friend said.

Small's heart skipped a beat.

"We're going to help you. We're part of an, organisation. We don't think boys should be kept from learning to read and write. We think things should be more, equal."

Small blinked at the two women.

"We thought you were sneaking the books home to your grandfather; a man of his age should be able to read. We were hoping to gain his trust through you and Farra and recruit him. We had no idea he had already taught you how to read."

Small was still too scared to answer. What if this was all an elaborate ruse to get him to come clean about reading and about Grumpa?

"We're not trying to trick you Small. Think about it. We're putting our own lives at risk here. You are as dangerous to us as we are to you right now."

Small tried to speak around the galloping heart in his throat. "Why would women help us?"

The librarian looked like she was about to start crying, "Because we're not all like that, Small, we don't all think you belong in the house working for free or working for next to nothing in menial jobs. We believe men can be just as clever as women; there's so much history and literature to back it up. Have you ever heard of a man called William Shakespeare?"

Small shook his head.

"He was this amazing poet and writer, and they just wrote him out of history. They still use his stories, but they just don't acknowledge him as the author, either saying it's by an unknown author or crediting his wife, Anne Hathaway, with his work."

"Oh, I've heard about her," Small said, looking at the women brightly.

"Of course you have," the librarian said, giving Small's chin a little squeeze.

Small felt the change, in the air inside him; he knew he was in it now, in his own amazing story. He was the heroine in this adventure, the brave youth trusted with great secrets by an exclusive underground society. Did they have code words and secret knocks? Would he find himself on unexpected voyages?

Small straightened his thin frame and raised his chin. "What can I do to help?" he asked.

EPILOGUE

Writing is a lonely job –

By Ester Spiller

originally written for SO:write women group

"Writing is a lonely job. Having someone who believes in you makes a lot of difference. They don't have to makes speeches. Just believing is usually enough."
— Stephen King, *On Writing*

It is a funny thing, isn't it? This part of ourselves we call creativity. It is, arguably, the very soul and centre of what makes us human. We create, we dream up, we make new.

Where I grew up there were these amazing weaver birds, with only their feet and beaks the male birds would weave intricate, beautiful nests. To me, every single one of them always looked perfect. The female weaver birds, however, were harsher critics. After the male painstakingly built the nests, the female birds would sometimes destroy them, and the male birds would have to start again from scratch. We were always told that the female inspects the nest, and if it is not to her liking, she rips it apart. Later, scientists found out the truth is that if the female isn't ready to lay her eggs yet she destroys the nest, otherwise it could get infected with pests before she moves in, putting her young at risk.

Whenever I write I think about those weaver birds, finding the right bits of foliage to weave together, working so diligently to create this thing I think is good enough, just to rip it apart later. Look, I know it needed to be ripped apart, because it wasn't ready, but there is still sadness in the destruction. It needed to be destroyed and rebuild until it is ready, until it can hold and protect the eggs of story and structure and plot and character and all the worlds of promise they contain.

Generally, like the weaver bird, we make new, alone. We fret and tinker and hope and fret some more, and sometimes, after much *MUCH* more fretting, we go out into the world and we shyly fold out our hands and say, "Look, I made a Pretty."

And the world scoffs and everyone pulls out their red pens and tells us not to start sentences with *but* or *so* and, if we're lucky, gives us a solid C and tells us how much more brilliant Faulkner was and in a barely audible whisper we say, "But I never wanted to be Faulkner, I just wanted to show you my Pretty."

And then doubt slinks in, it tells us that we're certainly not even nearly good enough, and although we keep on making Pretties we leave them in folders on our laptops where we hope they invite each other out for dates, or at least meet for coffee once a month, because *we're* lonely. So, we imagine *they* are too.

What we didn't know is that we needed a tribe. A gathering of like-minded people that also can't help but play with words and dress up characters and try to breathe life into the fragile flames of a new idea, hoping it will catch light.

Sometimes we just need to share our Pretties with someone, even before they are completely finished and while the glue is still drying, we just need someone to say, "Wow, look how good you are at making Pretties, I especially like the iridescent horns and how you made it smell like peaches."

And that is what I found here. A little tribe of writers. Some warriors, some weavers, some witches with words, and we tinker away, each making our own Pretty, and we discuss, and we encourage, and we support. And we never, ever, give anyone C's, or A's. And we never, ever, say Faulkner was better, because Faulkner is Faulkner and we are who we are, and if even Stephen King needs someone to believe in him, who are we to try and go at it alone?

www.ingramcontent.com/pod-product-compliance
Lightning Source LLC
LaVergne TN
LVHW041036150826
845672LV00001B/346

* 9 7 8 1 8 3 8 3 7 3 5 0 4 *